*RESET EARTH

Table of Contents

*RESET EARTH

The planet will always survive – man may not.

London.

February 9th.

Edna Jackson was tired, so very tired. She had never known anything like it in all her eighty-eight years. Edna lived alone in her top floor council flat in Hackney. Widowed for more than ten years, she kept herself to herself. All her old friends had either passed on or were in council run homes elsewhere. She hadn't seen anyone since she'd visited her best friend Mary in the care facility in Brixton. But that was in late October. It took three buses to get there, which she hated. What she hated even more now was leaving her own flat. The tower block had been virtually taken over by bad types – drug dealers, prostitutes, all sorts of criminals. She hadn't set foot outside the small flat since just before Christmas when she went to a service at the local church.

Her daughter, Rita, lived over two hundred miles away and phoned Edna almost every day. She also arranged for Edna's shopping to be delivered straight to her door by Asda once a week. Rita thought that was safer than Edna trying to venture out and going down on those disgusting lifts to the local shops. The last time Rita had visited, the lifts had dirty used needles on the floor and had smelled very badly of stale urine. She had emailed the local council to complain but no one seemed to care that her mother was living in a slum after working and paying tax most of her adult life.

Even though it was only early February the weather was very hot. A heat wave had started three weeks previously, on Christmas Day of all days. Temperatures unknown in the British Isles at that time of year were stifling the inhabitants of the entire country. In fact, the same was happening all over most of Western Europe too. The Met. Office were at a loss to explain it. The climate change fanatics were thrilled, of course. They were all happy that they were seemingly right about everything, justifying all those pathetic protests. All those gobby teenagers being used as mouthpieces for a bigger agenda beamed into cameras and winking at the gullible public.

It wasn't 'climate change' though. It was something much bigger and catastrophic, but no one knew how bad things were going to get at that time, early in the year.

Edna sat in her flat watching boring daytime television with a big fan that Rita had bought her blowing air at her. It didn't really cool her, it just recycled the warm air around the room at a furious pace. All the presenters on the television looked fed up and their gloomy personas flowed from the screen like a bad smell. The news was just as depressing. Three weeks into the freak weather and all the 'experts' the TV stations could find were at a loss. Yes, it may be climate change, they said, but it was happening too fast to be what they called a natural cycle of extreme weather. Never in all recorded history had it been this hot in the early months in the British Isles. Thirty-five degrees Celsius before March was even in sight and the temperature was rising by the day. When would it ever end? That was the question everyone wanted answering. Would the country end up as a scorched, desolate wasteland? People had had enough already and they feared what the summer would bring. They were all hoping for rain as usual.

Edna felt very lethargic. The small freezer that her daughter had bought her barely had time to freeze the bowl of water that Edna placed on the table in front of the fan before it could be rotated with its twin that had melted within half an hour. Edna couldn't find the energy to get up to make a nice cup of tea although she wondered why she would even consider putting hot liquid inside her. She hadn't even been eating more than bread and jam for the last few days. It was far too hot to even pop a ready meal in the microwave let alone eat a piping hot lasagna, shepherd's pie or a hotpot. It was even a struggle to get out of her chair at ten to move to the bedroom which felt like an oven. Sometimes she just slept in her chair with the fan constantly wafting a warm breeze over her. God knows how much her electricity bill would be this month. Would her meagre pension even cover it? It must be the same for more than half a million pensioners around the country.

Several hours later the landline phone rang for the third time. There was still no answer. Rita on the other end was starting to worry. She knew her mother wouldn't be foolish enough to venture outside. Not only was there a danger from the scumbags who occupied the flats but the heat out there was getting to dangerous levels, especially in the cities. She thought at first that Edna's phone could be out of order. She knew that London had been having brown-outs with the electricity supply. But the phone had been ringing. Would she hear the repeated ring tones at her end on the line if the power was down in her mother's flat? She wished she'd insisted on the mobile phone she wanted to buy for her mum, but Edna was a bit of a technophobe and refused the kind offer. She decided to try again in an hour.

***

London.
February 10th.

Steve Hansen was getting ready to record his latest almost daily podcast. He was one of the thousands of Youtube celebrities to give his views to the nation and was doing pretty well out of it. There was always some sort of scandal or wrongdoing out there, and London, where he was based, was possibly the worst of all places to live. Soaring crime rates, corrupt politicians, corrupt police... probably corrupt fishmongers and chimney sweeps too!

It was certainly not the city he'd grown up in and certainly not the sort of place his parents and grandparents had lived either. London had become a third world shithole. There was no denying it anymore.

Steve was getting close to forty-two, although he's been thirty-two to everyone but his closest friends for several years. He looked good for his age though, tall and slim with a mop of black hair over a face without the lines a man of his age should have, especially as he'd gone through a rather stressful divorce a few years previously. He'd lost pretty much everything, so decided to relocate back to London from York and try a different line. An old friend, Peter Marshall had called him and asked if he wanted to invest in his planned Youtube venture. Peter was an ex-BBC tech-head who wanted to start broadcasting on his own channel, on his own terms. He'd seen how the mainstream media had been suppressing the real events and spinning the news to fit their own agenda and was angry that the public were being lied to by the very people they were paying, via the licence fee, to bring them the truth and the real news. He decided enough was enough so initially wanted Steve to help with backing him up financially and also to be his cameraman/sound recordist. Turned out that when Peter was in front of the camera during test footage, he got very nervous and tongue-tied so suggested Steve gave it a go. Steve was a natural. He had the sort of easy-going personality that people trusted and was very at ease in himself, and his slightly dark sense of humour shone through to the public. Six years later it was great. Steve had over half a million subscribers

– mostly in Britain but many from all around the world too – all wanting the truth the media refused to broadcast now.

"Afternoon all, my good people. Phew, what a scorcher, as they used to print every summer on the front page of daily rags masquerading as newspapers back in the day. I went to the local sports centre today to cool down in the pool and guess what? It's closed - totally empty! Drained of all the water. Gawd knows where they drained it off to? Probably sold it off to France for drinking water because they've probably lost their bottle again. Hands in the air in surrender already and the Germans haven't even crossed the border yet. Half of Europe is suffering this weather too, so at least we can be sure it's not just us and it's not yet more retribution for daring to vote for Brexit. I just don't get it, and apparently neither can the brains trust of scientists we pay millions of our taxes to because they say they have to save the planet and we're to blame by using the crap plastic bags we get from Sainsburys or Tesco. Well, why don't they make them super thick like they were in the sixties and seventies so we can bloody well re-use them instead of kicking our tins of beans around the supermarket car park because the thin bags break as soon as you get out of the big sliding doors? Pete's nodding behind the camera – he had a similar experience outside the Ann Summers shop the other day. He's not stopped blushing since. Anyway, enough about Pete's embarrassment. I don't want to give him the hump because it's his round... assuming we still have enough water left in this country to make a few pints of lager. So, if anyone has any good ideas to help the boffins out of their embarrassing predicament please leave a comment below the video. How long will this last anyway? The average temperature has been rising at the rate of one and a half degrees Celsius a week for the past few weeks – Pete tells me it's almost thirty-one out there at the moment – I've no idea what that is in old money – got to be close to a hundred, isn't it? Pete's nodding again. Not sure if he's agreeing or he's dropped off to sleep. It has to be near siesta time for the old boy. I've been hiding in the shadows myself, trying to keep cool. Let me know what you guys are doing to stay frosty in the former traditional month of frost and ice. This reminds me of the old Brit Sci-Fi The Day The Earth Caught Fire with the bloke who played Rumpole of the Bailey and the actor who ended up doing the Think Bike! adverts on TV in the eighties, I think. In the film, some American and Russian scientists, unbeknownst to each other, had set up nuclear tests at the very same moment on different continents and the earth started to move closer to the sun, thrown out of orbit or something. I remember a lot of sweating and fog

and dear old Michael Caine doing a bit part as a copper. They don't make 'em like that anymore. Hopefully our scientists haven't been playing silly buggers and done the same thing... you never know though. To be honest I don't really believe in this 'climate change' nonsense. I read somewhere that the world has always gone through cycles of climate. We've had many droughts and a massive ice age in the past and pollution wasn't to blame for them, was it? It's all natural in my opinion, and all of us being taxed to buggery for it is just wrong in my opinion. The governments are perpetuating this climate hoax to drive us all into poverty so they can control us even more. Anyway, enough of the conspiracy theories that usually turn out to be conspiracy fact. Time I was off, good people. I'll catch you all tomorrow, assuming us or the equipment in our makeshift studio hasn't melted by then. Maybe I'll do it from a cold bath. That could be interesting. Probably get me de-monetised, though. See ya!"

"That was great, Steve," said Pete Marshall. "I'll get that ready for upload and then we'll have a pint, mate."

"Cheers, Pete. I noticed one of the spotlights was flickering a bit. I'll check it out while you're sorting things, probably just the bulb though. Lucky it didn't blow during my words of wisdom or we'd have to re-do a section and you'd have a bit of work editing before you upload. I think it all went pretty well. Let's get cracking and then get those drinks before Barry down at The Bull runs out of lager."

"I'm glad you left out the bit about Herren Gruppen Fuhrer Groot von Thunderbug being happy for once, Steve – she'd probably sue us. That will keep her in Primark socks for about three months the way our bank account is looking," Pete grinned.

***

London.
February 12th.

Edna had wet herself again. She just couldn't find the energy to get from her chair to the toilet more than twenty feet away. She felt very ashamed. She hadn't done that since she was seven or eight and soiling her sheets almost every night. It brought back bad memories of her poor mother having to change the bedding and telling Edna it was nothing to be worried about and everyone does it when they were little. Edna closed her eyes and tried to think back to better times - her wedding to Alf, the birth of Rita, her only child. She wanted more children but it was never to be. Having a job at Woolworths and her many friends and a nice life. Not stuck up on the top floor of a block of dingy flats as she was now. They'd had a proper house in Ealing, good friends and good neighbours too. It was a nice two up, two down near the shops with a decent sized garden front and back. Alf was a keen gardener and veg was grown at the back and a few flowers and shrubs for all the world to see at the front of the house. It was heaven compared to where she was these days. She missed her old life and her old friends so much now. Not many left now though.

She'd hoped that Rita would ask her to move in with her but she had her own family now - a husband, Brian, and two teenage boys, Ryan and Alex. There just wasn't the room in the three-bedroom terraced house in Torquay. She'd been to visit a couple of times and she'd loved the area but unfortunately it was just impossible to be made permanent. She was sure Rita and Brian would welcome her there if they possibly could, maybe when the boys went to university. She felt sad that she would probably die in this flat and wouldn't be found for days afterwards, rotting and stuck to the fabric of the chair. Maybe rats would get in? Just like that James Herbert book.

Edna wondered why Rita hadn't called her for a couple of days. Maybe she was busy at work. People ringing in sick because they couldn't face another day in a stifling office, packed like sardines in little booths trying their best to sound cheerful on the phone to their customers while feeling like battery hens, sweltering and starting to smell. Rita hated her job in the bank call centre but she was good at it and made a lot of money in bonuses, selling premium bank accounts with a monthly charge for very little benefit. Edna just had a normal bank account for her pension to be paid into and Rita had access to that online so she could take the money for the shopping Rita had delivered to her mum. Sometimes she wouldn't take the cash until Edna badgered her enough to do it. She was a good girl - even when she was a teenager. She worked hard at school and never played up too much.

Edna had about £200 in cash for emergencies but she hadn't used any of it and had spent the last of her change when she had visited Mary in the care home months ago. Even then the bus driver let her off for the seven pence she was short for her return fare. Nice man. Not many about these days, she thought.

She was lonely – there was no getting away from that and she wished she had a pet, a little dog or a cat to keep her company. She tried to pass the time and think of what name she'd call her pet but could not focus properly. It was hard to think through the stifling humidity. Her head started to throb. She had to get up for a drink of water, maybe even a sandwich. She still had some cheese slices in the fridge and she hoped the bread hadn't gone off.

She pushed her frail body from the chair and staggered towards the small kitchen. She held tightly to the back of the sofa as she shuffled. She closed her eyes for a moment and took a deep breath. The air was hot and stale outside the range of her fan. Edna felt faint and hoped it would pass in a few seconds. She stood gripping the sofa with her badly arthritic hands and then her legs suddenly gave way. She hit the floor, the thin carpet not doing much to cushion her fall and she lay unconscious, oblivious to the damage she had done to her hip and arm.

***

London.
February 14th.

"Afternoon all, Steve Hansen here again. Happy St. Valentine's Day to you all. Pete did give me a card - slightly worried now. Anyway, how are you all coping? I bet you are all sweltering as much as I am. By heck, these spotlights shining down on me to make me look even more beautiful than I really am don't make things any easier. I'm roasting in here. Pete won't let me have a fan on while we're recording because it makes my luxurious hair look like I'm a Greek god or goddess and we can't have dear old Pete feeling inadequate, can we? He gets enough of that at home. Anyway, Pete's woes and inferiority are not why you've clicked on the video... well, maybe one or two of you did. Talking of woes, have you noticed how the media loves a victim – especially if they are celebrities? I saw a few of the poor dears moaning about the heat and how it's affecting their mental health but the point is it's all done for sympathy and publicity. There is no reason why these people can't nip off to somewhere cooler, like Hell for instance. What really gets me is that all those little loves are millionaires and have the money and the freedom to jet off to Iceland or Canada or one of the many countries that hasn't been affected by this freak weather yet. They haven't got a solitary thought for anyone else, have they? Those who work forty or fifty hours in an office or a shop or outdoor workers digging up the roads in the baking sun. What about their mental health? Don't they matter? The ordinary people who do their best trying to keep this country functioning from day to day. All the while these celebrity nonentities are going boo-hoo! Look at me and how I suffer in my two million quid mansion with a swimming pool. I'd bet if they were allowed slaves to waft them with palm leaves all day long, they bloody well would. As long as the media didn't find out. Thanks for the comments yesterday by the way – especially the ones suggesting what you would do to keep cool. One subscriber, I won't mention his name, advocated doing things with ice cubes that my dear old mum would never approve of. And anyway, they wouldn't fit, mate. Time for me to have a little lie down with a wet flannel over my face because it seems the supermarkets are running out of bottled water, soft drinks and beer and cider. Well, they say they are and judging by their websites there is

no chance of getting any of these liquids delivered. Is this really the case or are they being stockpiled in case a celebrity drops in? Catch you all tomorrow, good people – maybe the bad ones too. Be safe and don't forget that sunblock. Let's be careful out there, as the man used to say on that cop show."

***

Wiltshire.
February 15th.

Rita was racing in her Hyundai up the A303 from Torquay in the early hours of the morning, she was understandably worried sick about her mum. They hadn't spoken for six days now and the phone just kept ringing in her ear – either not being picked up or there was a fault. British Telecom said there was nothing wrong with the line, of course. Rita had called the police two days ago but they had not called her back. Probably never even visited the flat. Too busy fining motorists for parking an inch on a double yellow line or playing music too loudly, maybe even for buying too much water that was becoming an expensive commodity just recently. Don't worry about all the shootings and stabbings, especially where her mum lived – just make sure the revenue stream isn't broken, she thought. At that moment she didn't really care about being caught speeding – her mum was more important than the fine and the points on her licence. She's probably only have to do a speed awareness course if pleading her case as an emergency failed.

Rita had left at 2 a.m. Knowing the journey would be a lot cooler and the roads less busy. The freakish hot weather was affecting everyone so badly, another reason she worried about her mum in her top floor flat in Hackney. Even in the early hours she had the air con in the car turned on to full, the cooling breeze blowing directly at her face and helping to keep her awake and focused on the road. She was close to Amesbury, having passed through a few towns she didn't recall hearing of before despite making this trip a few dozen times over the years, her mind was in a whirl. The journey was estimated at four hours on the Sat Nav but she could probably make in in just over three. There was hardly any traffic that early in the morning, just a few lorries making early deliveries to supermarkets and they were very easy to pass.

Rita was hogging the middle lane as usual when her car was buffeted by a BMW racing past her in the outside lane. It must have been doing well over 100 mph, maybe a lot more. She was doing eighty herself. She silently cursed them and switched the CD in the changer from Etta James to Marilyn Manson – she had a very diverse taste in music. From Heavy Metal to Opera - she loved it all and tried her best to sing along to take her mind off things.

Just before the Basingstoke turn off she hit the M3 motorway, pushing the small car up to a juddering ninety. All sorts of things were going through her mind now and she tried to block them out. She changed to CD player to Brahms to try and calm herself down. She wondered why the weather was so hot at that time of year. She should be more worried about snow and ice and not the bloody car overheating at gone four a.m. Rita glanced at the temperature gauge on the dashboard and it was rising steadily. He hoped she wouldn't have to stop and let the engine cool. The last thing she needed was to break down on the motorway, delaying her arrival at her mum's for an hour at least while she waited for the RAC to turn up. And by that time the car would have probably cooled enough to carry on her journey anyway. She had had the foresight to put a five litre container of water in the boot just in case as well as the drinking bottle in the cup holder in the centre console. That was already undrinkable because it had gotten so warm.

Certainly, this hot weather was not normal. What could be causing it? She knew people had been banging on about climate change for years but surely it should be a gradual change over a few years and not just hit Britain and most of Europe like this. She couldn't understand it. Maybe the government knew what was happening and refused to tell the general public? She chided herself for thinking like a conspiracy theorist but Brian, her husband, had shown her proof on the internet about events dismissed as conspiracy theories at first but later turned out to be true. Things like the MK-Ultra programme and the CIA testing LSD on some unsuspecting subjects and even controlling the weather through cloud seeding, HAARP and many other ways – it was all true in the end. Even the Dalai Lama was proven to be a CIA agent (or was it asset?) at one time. Could some foreign government be controlling the weather now? Rita tried to think of a few countries that were not being affected by this sudden heat wave at all and came up with the usual suspects – Russia, China and North Korea. Did they have that sort of technology available? If they could do this then what else could they do? Could all this lead to the end of civilisation as we know it? Now she was not only worried about her mum but her whole family too. *Shit! Calm down*, she told herself.

She swerved again as she lost her concentration. *Keep your mind on the job, Rita. You can't check on mum if you are in hospital or worse!* The engine temperature gauge was rising a little faster now – not far off the red. She prayed the car would be okay to reach London. The miles went by so slowly it seemed, even though she was doing a constant seventy-five to eighty. She had to slow a bit as she came to the outskirts of the city. It was now approaching 6 a.m. and the traffic was getting more congested the further she travelled and the car's temperature kept rising. She wondered what sort of people had to drive to work at that time of morning.

Rita finally reached the block of flats just before seven and parked in the quiet street opposite. The temperature gauge was in the red and the car had been labouring for the last few miles but she had just made it there in one piece. What looked like over two hundred black bin bags were piled up outside of her mum's building. It seemed there had been no refuse collection that week, maybe the week before too. *Christ even the council bin men had downed tools. What was the name of that dopey M.P. over here in Hackney?* She made a mental note to email her and complain, maybe someone could help her with the long words. The huge pile of rubbish stank to high heaven and she held her breath as she skirted around it and made her way to the foyer of the dilapidated block. It was well overdue a refurbishment but she supposed there was never any money for that sort of thing anymore. Inside it didn't smell that much better but at least she could breathe a little easier now. Rita pressed the up button on both lifts, hoping they were a bit cleaner than the last time she'd visited. The one on the left arrived first and she took it. The lift was in a state as usual but she knew she had to put up with it. She certainly didn't want to try to use the stairs. They were not at all safe in her opinion. Various dodgy types seemed to congregate on every landing.

The lift chugged, clanked and groaned all the way to the top floor and she gladly exited it and made her way to her mum's door. She didn't bother knocking for once and used the spare key her mum had given her for emergencies. Rita slipped the key into the stiff Yale lock and slowly pushed the door open. "Mum?" she called. No answer. She could hear the TV was on. *Could she have gone out and forgot about it?* Rita then heard a faint pained groan from the front room and rushed in. Edna was lying on her side, not moving. Her lips were parched and Rita immediately went to the kitchen to get Edna a drink of tepid water. After Edna had taken a couple of sips Rita dialled 999 on her smartphone and explained that her mum had taken a fall possibly four or five days ago and she was scared to move her until she was checked out first. She gave her mum's address and her age, hoping her mum would be a priority at that age. She mentioned it may possibly have been a stroke. Whether it was or not, she hoped they would get their skates on just in case.

The paramedics arrived in their green jumpsuits over an hour later. A middle aged man who seemed to be the senior of the two, and a thin, pretty blond girl of around nineteen or twenty by the look of her. Rita was not happy with the response time but was told her mum *was* a priority but thousands of people had been taken ill from the heat in the city and they had got there as soon as it was humanly possible. Before they arrived Rita continued to give her mum sips of water and a couple of stale chocolate digestive biscuits while they waited. She talked to her mum constantly but the only response she got from Edna were weak groans. She wondered if Edna had really suffered a stroke. After the paramedics arrived and checked Edna out and hooked her up to two bags of fluids they told Rita that it looked like Edna had just fainted and taken a bad tumble. She had a suspected fractured hip and also her right arm may be badly broken judging by the small lump just beneath her elbow and she needed to spend some time in hospital. The arm wouldn't be much of a problem and the hip would probably need an operation and weeks of rehab but a specialist would do a complete diagnosis after an x-ray and maybe an MRI too. The senior paramedic assured her that it wasn't a stroke and that came as a massive relief to Rita. They then gave Edna some pain medication and after a few minutes gently lifted her onto a gurney the young girl had gone down to retrieve from the ambulance a few minutes before, braving the lift on her own.

The paramedics told Rita which hospital they were taking Edna to and asked if she was coming with them in the ambulance or would follow on. Rita told them she needed to make a couple of calls first and also secure the flat by turning off the gas and electricity and would hopefully be at the hospital in about thirty minutes. She first called Brian to tell him what had happened and that she may be away for a few days while the hospital helped her mum get settled. She'd stay in a hotel instead of the flat though. Rita told him that Edna may have to come and live with them for a few weeks while she recovered. Brian wasn't too pleased but under the circumstances he said it was probably best. Edna had no friends to help her anymore. She also asked Brian to call the bank to say she wouldn't be in for a few days and to ask for compassionate leave although it was unlikely she'd get it and would probably have to use a few holiday days but even that option was frowned upon by the people who made those decisions - anyway, bugger them. She was staying up here even if she lost money over it. She knew she wouldn't be sacked for being absent - she made too much money for them and at the end of the day that's all banks cared about.

When the flat was finally secured, she returned to the disgusting lifts and again pressed both buttons to go down. They both arrived almost together. The left hand one had two large black men in. They stared at her sucking their teeth. The right hand lift was empty but full of litter – burger cartons, cups with straws that probably held cola or milk shakes at one time... and a couple of used needles. She took the empty lift. When Rita reached her car she locked herself in and took a few deep breaths to calm herself before she drove to the hospital. While she waited she entered the name of the hospital into the Sat Nav and discovered it was nearly forty minutes away. She wasn't even sure that the ambulance had got there yet. *What is this city coming to?* We're not in England anymore, Toto, to paraphrase a line from her favourite film. She sighed and turned the key then checked the temperature gauge before setting off. She should make it... just. Because that forty minute estimate may be nearer ninety.

Wiltshire.
March 11th.

Vera Castle was angry - very angry. What was the world coming to? All her life she'd cared about the planet. People not so much. They were the ones who had caused all this climate change. It said so in the tabloid papers almost every day and she believed it all. She decided that she would be the one to make them change their ways. She'd always had her special ability to make things happen but now instead of punishing individuals who had hurt her she would do it on a much larger scale.

Ever since she was a small child she'd known about her ability, her power. She would make her toys move on their own but had kept it a secret, even from her family. As an adult she'd researched what she was and what she could do. Telekinesis, like that Carrie in the film. It could almost have been about her life. As a child other kids had treated her badly. Bullied her for no real reason other than she was a bit small for her age and quite shy too. Bullies were like that. They would pick on the weakest in the group although she was never really in a group and found it hard to make friends. At nearly sixty-five that was still the case. Still alone and unmarried. She's never even had a serious relationship.

She lived alone on a small farm in the middle of nowhere. Rural Wiltshire. She liked it that way. The only person who came to the farm was the paper boy and the postman but he only delivered things like council tax bills so he was rarely seen. No real letters or postcards from far off places, no birthday wishes. Sometimes she wished she was normal. Lived an ordinary life with a husband and children. Maybe it was a possibility once, long ago. Gerald had dumped her for another woman after he had tried to use her. He eventually realised that was a big mistake. Forty-three years in his grave, rotting and being eaten by worms. What was left of him when they had buried the pig? She had gone to his funeral and stood at the back of the church during the service and secretly smiled at what she'd done to him. He'd thoroughly deserved it.

Vera thought back to the day she'd discovered her full ability... and used it. She was nine and at junior school. Just minding her own business during a breezy spring lunch break. She sat alone on a bench away from the main buildings, and after eating her fish paste sandwich and an apple, she got her new book out of her bag. She loved to sit there and read in peace. It was an Agatha Christie. Maybe a little advanced for a nine year old but she was pretty intelligent and could understand the long words and also the clever the twists in the plots of these books. What happened next was burned into her memory forever, the actions, the words, the outcome. It made her even more of an outcast and was really the start of the rest of her life. Her reality had changed permanently.

Karen Mills, a big fat ugly thing, and her cronies walked towards the single bench. Vera didn't even notice them as she read and hummed a pop song to herself. Hey Jude by The Beatles. Her favourite band. Better than the modern stuff. All the other girls seemed to be into Sweet, T-Rex and the Bay City Rollers. The large group of girls stood menacingly in front of Vera. She finally noticed them and looked up and saw Karen are the front of them and knew it wouldn't be good news.

"Watcha doing, freak?" Karen goaded with a wicked smirk.

"I'm just reading, and I'm not a freak. Why can't you leave me alone, Karen?" replied Vera, her voice almost stuttering with nerves.

"Of course you're a freak, you look funny and you smell like old cheese. Can't you smell it? All of us can. That's why you don't have any friends. Not that we'd be your friend, even if you didn't smell," smirked Karen. The other girls chuckled, thankful they weren't smelly freaks and victims of Karen's wrath themselves.

"Leave me alone! I haven't done anything to you," said Vera, trying hard not to start crying. It came out as more of a whimper.

"Lucky for you being a freak isn't catching or you'd be in real trouble, wouldn't you? It would be a lot better for you if your mum moved you to another school. Like one of those schools for retards and nutters," grinned Karen. More chuckles from the group made Vera scan the rest of them. There were a couple of girls she tried to make friends with at first but they didn't want to know. Alice Brand even lived next door and her mum was friends with Vera's mum. She knew Alice hated her. She hated living in this town and did wish her mum would move again. But would it be any different anywhere else?

"Go away!" pleaded Vera. "I hate you!" She could feel the tears were only moments away. Her head was getting hot even though it was still March and the sun wasn't even out yet. She felt a growing pressure from inside her skull. Heat, so much heat now. She was starting to get scared.

Karen went too far this time. Vera felt a slap across her face. It really hurt because her cheeks felt cold from the chilly wind. The Karen sat her great bulk on Vera's lap and put her in a head lock. "Freak… freak, freak, freak." Then the rest of Karen's gang started chanting, "Freak, freak, freak."

"Oww, get off me, you fat cow!" screamed Vera. Hoping a teacher was near enough to hear her and come to her rescue. The rest of the girls spread out so the view from the main buildings was blocked.

"You shouldn't say things like that, Vera, I may get angry and *really* hurt you. Put you in hospital, how would you like that? Lying in bed with broken bones and having to pee in a bottle because you couldn't move at all?" Karen started to climb onto, and bounce, on Vera's lap, her vast weight crushing the legs of the much smaller Vera.

"Please stop, Karen. I didn't mean it. I just want to be left alone." The tears were starting to flow now and Vera was pleading for Karen to get off her. The weight was unbearable. "I'll ask my mum to move me to another school, alright?"

"We're going to beat you up so bad, Vera," grinned Karen with evil intent.

The heat and pressure in her head was now insufferable. What was happening to her? Was she having a stroke like what happened to her Gran? Granny Maisie couldn't talk or even feed herself now and was always wetting herself sitting in her chair or in bed. She smelled bad too. She asked God not to give her a stroke. She didn't want to be like Gran. She wanted Karen to get off her so much.

All of a sudden Karen flew off Vera's lap and collided with two of the other girls a few feet away. They ended in an untidy heap on the muddy grass. Karen looked at Vera with murder in her eyes. She slowly got to her feet. She stood there glaring and wondering how a skinny little runt like Vera could push her off like that. She decided she wanted to hurt Vera so bad for what she did. She wasn't hurt, just a bit muddy and dishevelled, but worst of all she was made to look stupid in front of the rest of her gang and that she could not tolerate. She couldn't let them see any weakness in her… ever!

Karen started to move forward and then she stopped. She felt a bit funny. She had a sudden bad headache. Her nose started to run and she used the back of her hand to wipe it. It felt thicker and warmer than normal snot and she looked at her hand. Blood! The little cow had given her a nose bleed throwing her off like that. Vera was really for it now! Karen took another step and stopped again. Something was slowing her down, a sort of resistance like she was inside a bowl of jelly. Karen hated jelly. She found it harder and harder to breathe normally and the blood flow from her nose had got a bit worse. What was happening to her? She wanted to kill Vera now. Was Vera making this happen to her? What else could it be other than that freak causing it?

Alice looked at Vera and then at Karen and the blood flowing freely from Karen's nose and down the light green school jumper. Alice always hated the pale green uniform they wore, said it looked like sick or baby poo. Alice got worried and pulled Karen away from Vera. She virtually dragged her towards the main part of the school to see the nurse. Miss Parker wasn't a real nurse, just a teacher who was in charge of first aid and rarely dealt with anything worse than a skinned knee or someone being sick in class. The rest of the girls glared at Vera and followed Karen and Alice back to the old red brick buildings. Vera felt relieved but what had happened? All she did was wish Karen would get off her and then she did. The pressure and heat inside her head started to lessen slowly until she felt quite normal again. Then she worried about what Karen would do to her next time. She wanted to talk to her mum about this bullying and wanting to move away but knew her mum would call her silly and the bullies would move on to someone else eventually.

The next day at school they were all in class when Mrs. Phillips, the headmistress, knocked on the door and slowly entered. The teacher, Miss Francis, who Vera loved more than anyone in the world, even more than Agatha Christie, stood and welcomed the headmistress and asked if there was something she could do.

"I have a short, and very sad announcement to make," she said, looking quite pale and worried.

"Oh dear. Of course, Mrs. Phillips, now pay attention children," Miss Francis asked as she sat quietly behind her desk again.

"Sorry to interrupt your lesson, boys and girls, but I have some very important news. Karen Mills took ill last night at home and was rushed to hospital. She's very poorly and the doctors and nurses are doing their very best to help her. Some of you know that she had a very bad nose bleed here yesterday lunchtime and was sent home by Miss Parker, who thought she would be fine after a rest, but Karen's mum called me just now to tell me about what happened last night. Karen started to bleed again from her nose and also from her ears so they called an ambulance and quickly took her to hospital. They gave her more new blood from a bag like you see on the television, but she's still very unwell and the doctors are a bit worried. So I want you all to pray for her when you go to bed tonight and hopefully she'll be back with us at school very soon," she smiled nervously. She thought Karen may never be back.

That evening Vera lay in bed. She hadn't prayed for Karen. She wondered if anyone else had bothered for such a nasty bully. She still had about twenty minutes until her mum would poke her head through the open bedroom door and tell Vera to turn off the light and get some sleep, so she concentrated on her book. Poirot had gathered all the suspects in a drawing room and was about to reveal the murderer using his superior detective skills. He really was a genius and she hoped she'd finish the book before lights out. She thought she knew who had done all the murders and was desperate to be proven right. She thought she may want to be a detective like Poirot one day.

That night Karen died in her hospital bed. The post mortem revealed several burst blood vessels in her brain. If she'd survived she probably would have had to go to the retard school she said Vera should go to. Mrs. Phillips announced her sad death the next day during assembly with tears in her eyes and a cracked voice. Several of the pupils cried too, even some of the boys. Vera didn't cry but she was silently wondering if it was her that had caused Karen's death, and if so, how?

Vera smiled now as she remembered her schooldays. She knew now that it *was* her who had caused the fat bully's demise as she'd been responsible for quite a few more deaths over the years. She had decided to act several months ago. She would do things on a much grander scale. Not only would it send a message to everyone but she would be testing her powers. She had planned what to make happen and where for at least a dozen sites. She gave Britain a Christmas heatwave at first to assess the full weight of her ability and then would move further afield to find the extent of her range across the globe. Australia would be the ultimate test, of course, but she'd start closer to home first. It was the start of a rollercoaster for the world and it would be impossible to get off unless they started to treat the planet with a bit of respect.

Outer Hebrides.
March 12th.

Angus McMillan had reached the ripe old age of sixty-eight, a big grizzled man of the sea. He'd lived on Lewis all his life and loved the island. Angus had never even ventured to mainland Scotland from his peaceful island in the North Atlantic. Angus loved his life. Married with two grown up boys, one of which, Alex, worked with him on the trawler and the younger one, Michael, had moved to just outside Aberdeen twenty years before and now owned a small garage with lone petrol pump just outside of the city. Between them they had given Angus and his wife, Moira, four grandchildren. Alex had two lovely girls and two young boys for Michael. Angus saw the girls every single day because they lived in the tiny cottage next to Angus' larger one in the small, quiet village of Portvoller. He doted on them like most grandparents do. They were his life. Angus had been working on the boats since he was thirteen, just after his dear old dadda had lost his life in one of the many big storms to have hit the islands over the years. Dozens of good men and a few good boats had been taken by the cruel sea just in his lifetime. It was just accepted as part of the life they had in the Western Isles. No one complained and they all took it for granted that someone would be lost most years. Angus felt that he'd never retire from the boats. Not unless he had an accident or the trawler was taken by a storm. He knew he was still useful even at his age. His old bones creaked a bit but he was still very strong for a man of his years. He'd known nothing else in his life and wondered what he would do if he was forced to retire from the boats. Maybe teach the next generation of trawler men.

He and Alex were sitting quietly, mending the nets they would need for the next night. It was just after ten in the morning and they'd had a long night. It had been a good catch too. Angus sat with his lit briar pipe in the corner of his mouth, puffing away every thirty seconds or so while Alex was telling him what the girls had been getting up to and how well they were doing at the small village school. Alex proudly told Angus how bright they were and what great futures they had. It would probably mean leaving the island one day. The youngest, Isabell wanted to be a vet so she'd need to go away to qualify and hopefully be back when old McGregor got too old to do his job as the only vet on the island. The other, Molly, wanted to be a nurse and help the sick, she'd be able to train at the hospital in Stornoway when the time came, hopefully not the mainland, though. Two lovely, perfect girls, Angus thought as his old fingers started to ache from the constant mending.

Angus heard a loud rumble in the distance. A storm was brewing, he thought, and was pleased to think he'd be in his bed when it eventually struck. The weather had been hot and dry for weeks and he though a storm would cool things down for a bit before summer officially arrived. They were almost finished mending the nets. Angus looked out to sea. A dark wall of cloud was on the horizon. There must be a strong wind behind it because it was moving towards the island pretty quickly. Angus told Alex to pack up the gear. He didn't want either of them to get soaked before they got to bed. When the nets were neatly folded away in the small shed they used on the quayside, Angus glanced back again as the cloud rumbled once more. It was really travelling, he thought. Time to get inside. The two men started to walk swiftly towards their whitewashed cottages, eager to get into their beds, dry and warm. Their wives would be doing the housework without disturbing the pair too much during the day. After ten hours on the boat and another two emptying the hold at the harbour and mending the nets they were almost exhausted. They were both looking forward to eight or nine hours of good sleep before they relaxed for a couple of hours, had a big hearty meal, and then got ready for another night on the boat. The rumble was nearer. The two men looked back again... then blindly ran for their lives.

The giant tsunami struck the Western Isles at 10:17 on Friday the twelfth of March. The Coastguard helicopters and lifeboats searched for any survivors for three days but very few of the islanders were found alive. Most were discovered floating or clinging to debris. The islands of Lewis, North and South Uist as well as all the surrounding smaller ones had completely disappeared under the water. Half of Skye was also submerged. A week and a half later thousands of bodies started to wash up on the coasts of mainland Scotland and Northern Ireland but nowhere near the total souls lost. Britain held a national week of mourning for the islanders. An investigation revealed that the tsunami had mysteriously failed to show up on any radar or satellite images until minutes before it had struck the devastated islands. There was no evidence of an earthquake on the sea bed to cause it as this was the usual cause. It had just appeared, without warning, and ravaged the island communities. The usual suspects blamed global warming, of course. Michael McMillan and his remaining family attended a mass memorial for the people of the Western Isles in Edinburgh. He'd lost his mum and dad, brother and sister-in-law and his two little nieces, as well as many childhood friends, to a freak of nature that had killed more than fifty thousand and crippled the main industry in the area.

The heatwave across Britain and the rest of Europe slowly levelled off and although temperatures had dropped they were still well above the average for late February to mid-March, but at least there was some respite from the searing sun, although many still feared what the summer would bring. More than a hundred thousand people in Britain and over two million in Europe had died directly and indirectly from the unusual heatwave. Countless thousands more would die from skin cancer over the next few years.

London.
March 13th.

"Morning, good people. Steve Hansen here again. Well, what terrible news we all had yesterday. An awful disaster in the Western Isles of Scotland. What a blow for everyone concerned and, of course, our thoughts go out to the friends and the families of all the victims. What happened there though? I'm really at a loss as to how a major tsunami hit those islands with basically no advanced warning at all. Not only is a tsunami, remember when we called them tidal waves? unheard of in the North Atlantic, but I thought there was all sorts of flashy technology being employed these days as an early warning system? I thought there were sensors on ocean beds all over the world and satellites and buoys to detect weather changes and things like that. Why was this not detected well in advance? After all, millions, if not billions, have been spent on all this technology so why was there no warning in this case? It was possibly the biggest natural disaster in the history of this country since the Ice Age. Can someone please explain it to me? I doubt the Government or the Met Office ever will. You can sort of believe this sort of failure in third world countries near to massive fault lines but not the peaceful islands of Western Scotland for God's sake. It's just crazy in my opinion.

I don't know about you but I think there is something serious going on with the weather at the moment. In fact the whole planet. The climate prophets and doom mongers like Gruppen Fuhrer Groot von Thunderbug and that actress who flies to protests across the world all the time will tell you it's all our fault. I accept that mankind is partly to blame for some of it. What really gets me is that some countries get away with the majority of pollution and yet it's allegedly civilised countries like Britain, France, Germany and the US who are made to pay for the prevention and clear up of it despite being some of the lowest polluters on the planet? Why are we being mugged off like that? Why is it OUR financial responsibility? Not really fair, is it? I'd prefer to see my hard earned go towards paying for a pint down my local, to be honest. It's even better if Pete pays, though. Over four quid for a pint. Old gits like me remember when it was a quarter of that... and a pound for a pack of smokes. Anyway, I digress, good people. That's not the cause of this tragedy. But what is? We've always had freak weather at some time or other. I remember heavy snow around Easter time when I was a kid. We were all sent home when we should have been doing our exams. But this year seems to be more freakish than any other and maybe more is to come, who knows? Pete's nodding away like those dogs you used to have on the back parcel shelves of cars. Were they called parcel shelves at all? My old memory has been fried by all the heat we've endured since about Christmas Day. Bloody hell. I'm having to drink water now we have a beer shortage. Obviously God is not a drinker, is He? Anyway, for those who believe and pray, can you ask for a few million pints of lager to mysteriously appear? That would really be a miracle and it's all in a good cause. The bloody water I'm drinking is probably contaminated by something. Sewage or radiation or whatever. I'm sure life was never this complicated and frustrating in the past.

And something else that springs to mind. Where are all these gobby celebrities who tell us all we are bad people? Why are they not putting their hands in their pockets? People who fly around in private jets and billionaires who are now taking trips into space? Hypocrites, every single one of them. But it's us normal people who suffer, isn't it? Taxed to the limit to get us all off the roads while the rich drive Bentleys and Ferraris with impunity! They don't drive the same car for twenty bloody years like I have because they can't afford to replace them. New car, boat, private plane for them every year – but WE'RE the bad guys and WE have to pay. I despair for us ordinary people, I really do. I would emigrate but where would I go? - everywhere is going the same way

At least the heatwave seems to have died down a little, so that's something to cling on to, I suppose. Next time I'll be highlighting the growing erosion of our freedom and civil liberties – it would take way too long to add that to this video today.

There will be a link under the video for a disaster relief charity in aid of the victims of the Scottish tsunami. Please give if you can but obviously no pressure. We all have our financial worries that need to be prioritised. Our families come first as always and that is the way it should be in my opinion. As usual, leave your comments and thoughts below. I do read every one of them. So stay safe everyone and I'll catch you all next time."

"Good one there, Steve," said Pete. Christ, what must it have been like for the victims up there? No one would have expected anything like that in that area. It's very chilling to be honest."

"Yeah, we all saw the pictures from Thailand a few years back, but the fact this was practically local brings it home a bit more," replied Steve. "Jesus, what is happening out there?"

"Do you think it is just climate change or something else?" asked Pete. "I've got a mate who swears it's all down the chemtrails and secret weapon testing."

"Ten years ago I'd have said your mate was a nutter, but now I'm not so sure," signed Steve. "Look at all those instances of tens of thousands of birds all dying at once or the whales and dolphins washing up on beaches. Something is certainly off and we have no idea what is going on at the moment. It scares the life out of me, to be honest, mate."

"I worry all the time, to be honest, but I won't say anything in front of the wife," said Pete. "Right, I'm going to get this lot prepped and uploaded. Meet you in the pub in about twenty minutes?"

"You read my mind. I certainly need one or two. With this beer shortage we may be on Babycham or bloody alcopops. See you in a mo, mate," smiled Steve.

Blackpool.
March 18th.

Henry Small sat in his dingy flat near the famous tower. He was fifty-five, and average height, but overweight. The single dusty light bulb reflected off his bald head. He couldn't admit to people that he was old and bald so he shaved his head, or more correctly got Mucky Mavis in the flat below to do it for him. Henry was officially disabled. Agoraphobia allegedly, but it didn't stop him going out and selling drugs to kids, the money used to fuel his own amphetamine habit. He was single but had got into trouble with the law when his controlling and bullying went too far with previous girlfriends. He'd spent time in prison in the past and was quite proud of that fact – a badge of honour, he thought. At his advanced age he realised he'd never find anyone decent and now spent his time playing video games, on porn sites and with Mucky Mavis, a worn out prostitute. The flat was always in a bit of a mess. Empty coke bottles and jaffa cake boxes littered the floor. He was too lazy to keep on top of the mess and 'allowed' Mavis to come and come in and clean once a week, usually on a Monday when she 'rested' after a busy weekend in the dirty, dark alleys of Blackpool.

Henry went out on his usual short walk to where the youths congregated, his pockets full of Class A pleasures. The streets were almost deserted, even for off-season March. He wondered what had happened to the usual bustle of the town. In the distance he could hear a faint drone in the air. He dismissed it. Nothing to do with him. He walked a little further off his usual route, wanting to make at least some money. Maybe hang around outside the rundown secondary school on George Street. Some of the kids there would do anything to score. Young boys as well as girls. He thought he heard faint screams, he could have been wrong though. He dismissed it. It could just be the wind coming off the sea and flittering through the filthy alleys of the dirty town he grew up in. He knew the wind sometimes made strange noises on the coast. There it was again. He looked up and saw the sky to the east quickly darkening. It looked like a giant heavy black cloud moving slowly towards the town. Henry had come outside without a coat and now didn't want to get soaked by the heavy downfall that looked to be headed his way so he started off back to his one bedroom flat. He hated it when the rain bounced of his flattish shaven dome. He quickened his pace, hoping he wouldn't have to try and run which caused his belly and man boobs to sway in several different directions. Embarrassing.

He definitely heard screams this time but hey were almost covered by an incessant droning. He looked to the skies and started to panic. What he thought was a dark rain cloud was a swarm of something. Bees or wasps maybe? Henry did start to run then. He hated wasps. He also knew that anyone who was stung enough times would die from the accumulation of poison from the stings causing a reaction that would stop you breathing. Anna Flitic shock? Others he saw were fleeing too, racing past him easily. He almost tripped over a child who had fallen and given up trying to escape. The small girl sat on the ground and cried until the swarm enveloped her. She screamed for a second or two and was then silent. Henry screamed too – he was utterly terrified. He, very wobbly, ran for his life.

Henry made it back to the flat. He had actually flung people roughly behind him to get in front of them. Women and children - he didn't care. All he wanted was to get safely home. Inside the flat he hid in the bedroom and wept uncontrollably. He prayed they wouldn't get in. He knew all his windows were closed because he had checked before he went out. Can't trust anyone these days, especially the drug addicts he supplied. Henry heard agonised screams coming from below. They had got to Mavis. Her windows must have been open. He didn't care as long as he was safe - screw everyone else. Henry remembered he'd heard that the recent heat wave had meant the wasps and other insects had been breeding more, especially ants. Was that the cause? He wasn't sure. He had never been the sharpest knife in the drawer. Was this happening all over the country? How the hell do you kill that many wasps? Will the army be issued a tin of Raid each? Gas! That was it. The RAF would gas them all from planes or choppers. That will kill them. Sod the people outside who would be exposed. Death by gas would be far better than being stung thousands of times by the evil little buggers.

Henry could hear louder droning. It was too close, he thought. They can't have got in. It was impossible! He plucked up whatever courage he had and cracked open the bedroom door slightly. Wasps. Everywhere! All over the tatty green furniture. He squealed, the girly scream constricted in his throat. The wasps were alerted to the sound and suddenly flew at him. He tried to slam the door but the force of several thousand of them battered the door back open. He staggered backwards onto the bed and was then covered in the yellow and black stinging insects. His exposed hands and face swelled out of all proportion. They stung at his wide eyes, blinding him. He tried to scream and his toothless mouth was filled with the creatures, his tongue and throat started swelling too. They burrowed deeply into his ears. He was paralysed, curled up on the bed. He could feel each individual sting from the thousands he suffered. The torture was totally unbearable. He wondered what would happen after he died, if there was an afterlife. He doubted he'd go there after the way he had treated the people in his life over the years. Henry died terrified and very alone. Maybe Karma did exist after all?

Westminster, London.
March 19th.

"Can someone please tell me what the bloody hell is going on?" shouted Robert Garland, the Prime Minister.

"Well, Prime Minister," replied Jonathan Banks, Minister for the Environment. "We do seem to have an unprecedented number of natural disasters in such a short space of time and we in my department are at a bit of a loss at the moment. Obviously these things happen from time to time, except the tsunami or course, but not all at once as is happening at the moment. Maybe it's just very bad luck?"

"BAD LUCK!" screamed Garland. "I can't run a country based on how bloody lucky we are! I want answers – and bloody well soon!"

"Sorry, Sir, what I meant was there doesn't seem to be any real plausible or natural explanation for it. The tsunami was a one-off freak event and there seems to be no particular cause or explanation for it. As, I'm sure you are aware, they are caused by earthquakes, normally on the sea bed, but there were no earthquakes anywhere that preceded the massive surge. There was absolutely no reason for it to happen and it was possibly the first tidal wave to hit Britain for hundreds of years. Yes, the recent heatwave could, in theory, be put down to climate change, but I don't think anyone could blame a colossal swarm of wasps attacking people on the climate. Maybe the heatwave did indeed contribute to the increased numbers of the wasps but not the reason they swarmed," said Banks.

"Keith, your thoughts?" said the PM.

Keith Kendall, Home Secretary, replied tersely. "I have to agree with Jon, PM. The tsunami was a freak event but the mystery is just why it wasn't detected. Even a few minutes warning could have saved many lives and I shall be reviewing the technology we have and will head the inquiry into its apparent failure myself."

"Good," said Garland. "Mike? Give me some good news."

"I wish I could, PM," said Michael Connor, the Chancellor of the Exchequer. "With the Budget announcement next week we're now in a bit of a panic trying to juggle things at the last minute. Insurance claims are through the roof, especially claims in life policies. The heatwave and the tsunami hit the industry very hard. I don't think there has ever been such a collective pay-out ever before. This means the companies will have to claw back all of that with increased policy costs, which is good news for us because I'll be adding two percent to the Insurance Premium Tax. I'm holding off on raising income tax for now but will review that decision before November. But the bad news is the effect of these disasters on tourism and trade. I doubt Blackpool will recover for possibly two or three years, maybe longer. The army made a bit of a mess—"

"Now hold on!" piped up Sir Miles Crawford, Minister of Defence. "The army did what they needed to do. One hundred percent absolutely. They saved lives. The situation could have been a lot worse if we hadn't authorised the use of chemicals to first disperse, and then kill the wasps. Yes, there was collateral damage to the health of the public but I'm sure they would have preferred that to a horrible death from thousands of wasp stings, don't you think?"

"Calm down, you two," said Garland. "Alex?"

"Yes, PM," said the Health Secretary. "The chemicals used in and around Blackpool will, in fact, place yet another burden on the NHS. As you know, the hospitals were at breaking point trying to cope with the effects of the heatwave. There are still hundreds of people hospitalised because of it, especially the elderly, and every GP in the country is swamped too. We still have no idea what the final death toll will be because people were advised to stay indoors and there could be thousands more victims who haven't been discovered yet," said Alex Peterson, the Minister for Health. "It's all a bit of a mess, to be honest, Sir."

"Thank you, Alex. I appreciate the strain your department is under," replied the Prime Minister. "Anyone else?"

"Obviously we've had plenty of sympathy from around the world," said Foreign Secretary, Anne Bowles. "As you know, most of Europe was just as devastated by the heatwave as ourselves and, understandably, cannot offer any assistance. Either financial or logistical. America is possibly on the brink of a civil war due to the alleged election fraud and have their own problems to deal with. The other big world powers know their economies will grow while Europe's declines. Canada and Australia are doing what they can, especially logistically. The rest of the world still has the begging bowl out, I'm afraid, and continue to rely on us even through our own difficulties."

"Thanks Anne, I assume you are in the process of cancelling all Foreign Aid? There will be a bloody revolution if the public see us continue to throw money at these people before looking after our own needs first," said the PM. "After all, we were all elected to govern *this* country and not those who harbour terrorists. We've given billions when other countries have suffered disasters – where is all the reciprocation when *we're* in need? They'll call us all racists but that's the usual response to not getting what they want now, isn't it?"

"Yes, PM. Top of the list," smiled Anne.

"All right, let's leave it there for now ladies and gentlemen," said Garland from the head of the long polished table. "I hope we're past all these disasters now and we can rebuild our country. Not only the devastation we have suffered, but the morale of the whole nation. I just hope the press stay off our backs a while longer and let us do our jobs."

London.

April 1st.

Steve Hansen was taking some time out to check his emails and do a little work, and life, admin. He deleted all the spam without even opening them - usual stuff, loan offers, phone deals and links to midget porn. One looked unusual to him though. There didn't seem to be a sender listed in the From box. That column in his email manager was strangely blank. He was intrigued. After first using his virus checker to scan for anything nasty and finding it safe he opened the email.

Mr. Hansen,

You need to read this and take heed of the message. I am Mother Earth. I have been causing the unusual weather patterns and other disasters in Britain and soon there will be major events in Europe and the rest of the world too.

NO! DO NOT stop reading and delete this message! You need to listen and inform your viewers and listeners about what is happening and what I am doing for the good of the planet we live on.

I am not causing these events lightly. People need to be shown that EVERYONE has to act to save this planet and no one will listen unless a few examples are made. I do feel sorry for the families of all the victims but these demonstrations of my power were necessary. The time for talking and false promises by governments is over, Mr. Hansen.

Another manifestation will present itself in the coming days in the South-West of England, followed by another major event in London. You will realise I speak the truth when they do happen. YOU must warn people. Tell them why these things are occurring. And meanwhile I will keep causing these catastrophes until everyone starts to listen and begins to ACT in the interests of our planet.

You will hear from me again after the next two events.
Mother Earth.

Steve chuckled. "Bloody nutters are coming out of the woodwork now. Another mental attention seeker."

He didn't delete the email though. He wanted to show it to Pete. Maybe his tech man knew how someone could send a message without leaving a 'from' address. It was certainly intriguing him now.

Pete arrived around forty minutes later and was completely stumped as to how the sender could stay so anonymous. You couldn't do it using a VPN or VPS - they only masked your location and could never really conceal the sender's identity completely. He did point out the date to Steve though and put it down to a very clever prank. They both chucked at the ruse but in the backs of their minds they both thought something was very off about the email.

"Morning, good people, and even the bad ones too. Even those who can't decide what they are. Pinch and a punch - first day of the month as we used to say at school as an excuse to bully smaller people. If any kids are watching then I have to stress that bullying is bad and cowardly... unless you want to grow up to be a politician or join the police. Pinch and a punch was the extent of my bullying at school because everyone else was doing it. It was sort of a tradition but it wasn't classed as proper bullying in those days. Now if you even fart in the wrong direction it's deemed a hate crime by some people, especially Mr. Plod.

Anyway, it's a double celebration, being the first of April. When silliness is allowed the world over, even in Russia... I wonder if they soak the raw onions they eat in vodka? I suppose it relieves the boredom and frostbite, doesn't it? Can you tell I'm in a silly mood?

April Fools Day used to be fun back in the day. I remember trying to spot the fake news stories in the papers, television and websites and having a chuckle, but now the world is so mad you can't tell the jokes from the real news, can you? Seems the fake news is more believable, which is a bit worrying to say the least, to be honest. There really is some mad stuff going on at the moment. I thought the news from Blackpool was a hoax at first until I saw video of the devastation up there caused by the wasps and then the measures used to kill them.

Older viewers may remember the 'spaghetti trees' one years ago. Has anyone spotted a good one today? I know I haven't. There was a story about Britain sinking due to the extra weight of all the illegals but I'm not too sure if it was a hoax or not. Maybe we should concrete over the gap between Britain and Ireland and build a few more houses for them? Oh God. I hope I haven't put ideas into the heads of this dopey Government although those idiots would probably join us to France instead. And we bloody well don't want that do we?

Back to today, though. I've had loads of emails from you crazy lot. Some were quite interesting. One said that the cause of all these disasters was aliens. The truth is out there... somewhere. You never know what the 'truth' might be though. I doubt the reason is banal. One email has asked me to tell you all that it's all our fault and we have to all be good and contribute to saving the planet. In my opinion we've all been bullied into doing our bit anyway... and we're back to bullying again. We all recycle, right? Or we should. We're paying more than ever for our fuel - gas, electric and petrol, aren't we? That gets a few more people off the road. Not because they want to save the environment - it's because they can't afford to bloody well drive anymore! I know I can't, but finding somewhere to park in London is even worse. Still our mental Mayor thinks he's doing the right thing by upping charges and stopping some cars getting into the capital due to their emissions but I do wonder how much his entourage of bodyguards in several vehicles is producing in pollution. I'm sure he's doing it all tax-free, unlike the rest of us. We're being 'encouraged' to buy electric cars but that still means they have to be charged by energy produced from burning fossil fuels - doesn't make sense right? And what's with all these electric cars suddenly bursting into flames spontaneously? Firemen will tell you these lithium batteries are a bugger to put out when they are in flames. And then you have these hybrid cars that not only have a highly combustible battery but a tank full of bloody petrol too! Anyway, that email said they were actually causing everything that has been happening this year. I presume they meant the winter heatwave and the tsunami. Well, it takes all sorts, doesn't it? I wonder what will be to blame next. Brexit?

So kids, remember bullying is just wrong because it's all about control at the end of the day and as my dear old Uncle John once told me - there is always a bigger bully than you just around the corner. Well, I'm off to look out of the window and wait for the aliens to come and save us. Have a good one people and keep your chin up - or chins in the case of my wing man, Pete."

"Dick!" said a grinning Pete. "I should edit that bit out."

"You know you'll leave it in," grinned Steve.

Minutes later Hansen received another anonymous email:

You really have to take me seriously, Mr Hansen. Heed my warning. Mother Earth,

Vera was fuming at Steve Hansen for making fun of her. He'll see that she meant what she wrote. They'll all see. She wondered just how long it would take, how many lives lost, before everyone wised up to what was happening and how long it will take for people, and governments, to act. She closed her laptop, rose from her kitchen table and prepared to go to work.

Cornwall.
April 4th.

The water started to seep slowly from underneath Bodmin Moor. Within an hour there was a lake stretching a mile in each direction of the source. Being a remote area no one noticed the swelling mass of brownish liquid until it was too late and it was already on the move.

Andy Parsons, a sales rep for a farm machinery company was driving on the A30 heading from Bodmin to Launceston. The direct route would take him over the desolate moor. He was thirty-eight and very single, not wanting to be tied down to anyone. He loved the life of pulling a different girl every week. He had the good looks and also the chat. Andy was always on the road, living from hotel room to hotel room, county by county. The commission he made was very good and the company paid his expenses, so most of what money he made was ferreted away and used on a couple of great holidays every year. Christmas and New Year was usually spent in Thailand and this summer he was booked in for a month in New Zealand. Travelling was always his 'thing' whether it was working in the UK or going abroad for fun and games. It was all very different from the cheap package holidays in Spain he and his mates went on in their late teens and early twenties. He was thinking of going to Mexico this winter and thought he'd check out a few locations on his laptop in the hotel room later on. His tales of travelling around the world always impressed the girls he chatted up. All the pictures too, when he got them back to his hotel room.

As he drove towards the moor he could feel a slight rumbling beneath him. He hoped it wasn't a problem with the car because being off the road would affect his earnings. The vibration got worse so he pulled over and got out of the car to check around the wheels and wheel arches in case he'd picked up a bit of debris somewhere, maybe a small branch or part of a bush. The vibration was still under his feet so it definitely wasn't the car and he breathed a sigh of relief. But what the hell was it? An earthquake? They were pretty rare in Britain and usually very minor so he wasn't too worried. Then he heard it. It sounded like a small waterfall in a placid garden pond. The sound grew louder and louder though, the tremors gradually increased. He was parked in a small isolated valley. The mounds of earth either side of the road rose around ten to twelve feet above him. He didn't have time for a last thought as the water cascaded into the dip, sweeping him into a vortex and smashing him violently against his own car. Andy's badly broken and lifeless body was swiftly carried away by the intense flow of water, followed by the severely crushed car.

The thick muddy water flowed south towards the coast, flooding the town of Bodmin itself and continued on to St. Austell, Fowey and Looe. The three coastal towns were lost to the sea, possibly forever. Thousands more lives were lost and close to eighty-four thousand more made homeless by the devastating flood and the map of Cornwall was changed, maybe for many years to come.

London.
April 5th.

"Good evening and welcome to BBC One's The Agenda, a programme full of diverse views presented by diverse people for a diverse audience. Tonight we are here to discuss the extreme weather the country, and most of Europe, has been suffering. With me tonight we have Professor Bernard Newey, a climatologist from Queens University, Belfast. Celebrated author Mark Mason, Dame Margot Brimmington-Taylor, government advisor on climate change, General Sir Tristran Hardacre, head of the government's Armed Forces Rapid Response Unit, and last, but not least, Steve Hansen, a Youtube personality who is gaining more popularity due to his unusual take on the whole situation."

The five guests sat at a semi-circular desk with the black female host, Ayah Shanise, looking like a panther ready to pounce in a black silk dress, her long hair woven in braids and beads. The panel faced an audience of around four hundred adults with five TV cameras set in between.

"So, if we can start with you, Professor Newey, can you bring us up to date with the terrible events so far?"

"Certainly, Ayah," he said, before clearing his throat as a camera formed a close up of him for the viewers at home. "As most people are aware, this year has seen some unprecedented weather patterns. Individually nothing unusual, of course, but collectively a disaster. Not only ecologically, but the financial impact could last months or even years before we can recover. The whole country and parts of mainland Europe have had a heatwave earlier in the year which claimed the lives, both directly and indirectly, of many thousands of people. The devastating tsunami hitting the West of Scotland too. Again, many thousands of lives lost. The very unusual wasp attack in Blackpool. We all know that wasps are prone to attack if they are agitated but such a gigantic swarm is virtually unheard of in this country. Several relatively minor events have been recorded all around the country too. Now, obviously most of these *can* be blamed on climate change, that's only natural, but all these events happening in the same year in such a short space of time... that is the main concern we

"

all have. As a lot of people know, a tsunami is usually caused by an undersea earthquake, but no earthquake was recorded anywhere near the Western Isles and so there was no warning for the unfortunate victims, absolutely no chance to evacuate any of them. Now this is a massive worry for us all. It obviously could be viewed as a freak event, a one-off, but what if it's not? We need to find out just why there was no warning for a start. Did all the undersea recording apparatus fail? If it didn't then we need to discover exactly how and why a tsunami formed itself without any apparent seismic disturbance. Above all, we have to avoid any panic from the general population, that's really the last thing we need right at this moment. Although it's obviously not my field, but I would say panic buying, hoarding and the like would make things exponentially worse for everyone. Possibly an epidemic of malnutrition if the less well-off families don't have access to basic foods because of a national shortage. Maybe one of the other guests is better qualified than me on those sort of problems, you know, the health side of it."

"Thank you, professor," purred the feline-like presenter." Dame Margot, what has been the government's response to the disasters, so far?"

"Well, obviously, no blame can be attached to the government at all. Yes, there have been freak events outside their control but official policy dictates climate change is definitely to blame. For years, we, as in the advisors to successive governments, have been warning of such events. Floods and droughts all over the world are usually predictable but there is just not the money available to combat these events anymore. Obviously, a lot of them happen in poorer countries and the richer ones like the UK, US and some in Europe have had to foot the bill in the past but the coffers are running dry, so to speak. But in turn, the inaction has made things worse, especially when some countries, and not just poor ones, do nothing and indeed make the problem exponentially worse every single year. What we have always proposed is a global taxation, with those countries more at fault paying more into the fund to fight climate change while we still can. Before it's too late. If these countries who cause most of the pollution get away with not paying their share then they will certainly continue what they are doing with impunity. In theory it could lead to increased global tensions and maybe even war in my opinion."

"I think we can all agree that this is no longer a long-term problem," said Professor Newey. "But is taxation really the answer? This tax will be passed onto ordinary people who are already doing what they can and are barely surviving financially. No! It is up to entire nations, in my opinion, but as you intimated - some just aren't playing ball with the rest of us and that makes it almost impossible to effectively combat the issue."

"What do you suggest, Professor Newey?" asked General Sir Tristran Hardacre. "Threaten them with war if they don't comply? Risk a World War Three? If we did that there would be no planet left to save, for God's sake!"

"No, not war, but firm economic consequences, sanctions that will keep them in line and on the same page as the rest of us," replied the professor. "Hit them where it really hurts - in the damn pocket!" stressed the professor bluntly.

"Poppycock! That could lead to war as well. You know the sorts of regimes that rule these countries, totalitarian states only interested in themselves. And you are forgetting that we need those trade agreements just as much as they do. No - it's foolish idea, in my opinion," said the general.

"Mr. Hansen. What's your take on the crisis?" asked the presenter. "I hear it's pretty unusual, some may say it's a bit fanciful and 'out there'," invited the presenter, leaning forward slightly in her comfortable chair.

"Well, yes - some may find it fanciful, or even a hoax, as I did at first," offered Steve. "But what has been happening to me, and I'm not sure if others have been contacted, is this. I've been getting emails from someone or something claiming to be Mother Earth. The emails can't be traced and have no sending email address and it's impossible to reply to them. They come from who knows where and warn us all of the dangers of destroying the planet. The thing is, this 'Mother Earth' says the disasters were have faced are deliberate and are warnings and have even predicted the next attack on us. Ice! Just as the heatwave earlier in the year was out of place, heat instead of cold, then as we are almost in summer we will get devastating, coldness... ice storms, possibly, I'm not sure. The emails from this apparent entity warn we have to act now to avoid many more catastrophes, and they will also spread worldwide. Millions, if not billions people are at risk of death, injury or displacement. That's just my opinion, of course. I'm trying to keep an open mind at the moment. Now, I don't know why I have been contacted by whoever has sent these emails. Well, a possible reason - they are dire warnings - but why me? I can assure everyone watching that this is not a publicity stunt or hoax to get more hits on my channel or advertising revenue. I'm genuinely freaked out by all this.

It could definitely be supernatural in my view! I just can't see anyone having the technology to cause these disasters to be honest. Maybe the general can enlighten us on current technology to kill and maim people."

General Hardacre glared coldly at Steve Hansen. *If looks could kill,* thought Steve.

"And talking about the supernatural, we have the horror author Mark Mason on the panel, a man apparently well versed in supernatural events. He was originally here to promote his new book, Second Chance, at the end of the show but my producer persuaded him to come onto the panel and give us his thoughts of the phenomenon you are experiencing with these email warnings and predictions from this Mother Earth."

"Yes, thank you, Ayah. As you said I was invited to talk about my new book, which is available at all good bookstores and a few bad ones too," he grinned. "On a serious note, yes, I'm well versed in the supernatural, both through my books and in real life. Strange things do seem to happen to some people, although most aren't very receptive and pass things off as coincidence or weird anomalies, that sort of thing."

"So what is your take on what Mr. Hansen has revealed?" asked the presenter.

"I'm intrigued. Well, to be honest, I believe him. I understand that your production team will show your audience the actual emails both at home and in the studio. Yes?"

"That's right, Mr Mason, can we put them up now?" the presenter asked the director.

A slideshow of the emails then appeared on giant screens above the heads of the studio audience and on screen for the viewers at home.

"As you can see," continued Mark, "there is no 'from address' on any one the emails. As far as I'm aware, and maybe the general can either confirm or deny this, but an email has to have a source to send from and it's impossible to hide that and can always be traced - and it's blank as you can see." The general nodded his assent curtly. "Now, what if these emails *are* actually from this 'Mother Earth'? What if the sender really is a supernatural entity and it's not some clever hoax, what then? What do people do? Would they actually believe in some supernatural representation of the planet, like the fabled Gaia, or continue to ignore the warnings until the entire world population is extinct? By then it really would be too late, wouldn't it? I know some people are advocates of a total reset of the whole planet. It's happened in the past, plagues, asteroids, ice ages, floods and so on. Are we really prepared for something like that now? Is everyone so ignorant of the consequences and the actual increasing timescale of these disasters? I don't want to sound like a fanatic, or even a touch melodramatic, but we really need to act, and very soon. It will be very interesting, and more to convince the public and governments alike, if the prediction of an anomalous ice event did happen this summer. I'm already convinced that this is *not* a hoax, Ayah."

"Thank you, Mr. Mason," smiled the presenter, trying to hide her scorn for both the writer and the Youtube presenter, who were both more popular than she was.

At that moment a loud repeated banging, like a bass drum, was heard in the studio. Guests and audience alike started at each other and then at the studio ceiling, wondering what was happening above them.

"As our viewers can hear there seems to be some kind of disturbance, possibly from outside the building. I don't know where it's coming from exactly but it does sound like it's coming from above our heads," said the presenter straight into the camera in front of her. "We'll try and find the cause and hopefully deal with it quickly. Meanwhile, I'd like to ask General Sir Tristran Hardacre what exactly the procedure is for his Rapid Response Unit. Are they on constant standby and where? Do you have several locations around the country on high alert, and has that alert status increased or escalated in recent months or are they always ready for any eventuality like major terrorist attacks, for example."

"Ah, well, yes, Ayah. Obviously I can't reveal exactly where the various units are stationed, National Security and all that, you know, but yes, they are constantly on alert for any emergency in this country and are a maximum of one hour away from any location as, and when, they are needed. We pride ourselves on our response times." The general smiled nervously and sporadically looked towards the roof of the studio as the intensity of the banging increased, both in volume and frequency.

Then, the unthinkable happened. I giant block of ice, about twenty feet square, crashed through the studio roof. Mark Mason pushed Steve to the side and then followed him in the same direction. Being on the end of the panel saved their lives. The others were not so lucky. The professor, general and government advisor were killed instantly by massive slab of frozen debris. The presenter was trapped underneath it, not only the crushing weight on her lower half but the extreme cold slowly killing her, quickly lowering her body temperature. She screamed in agony and then fortunately for her, passed out. There was a panic amongst the studio audience and the camera crew and many more died in the crush as everyone piled towards the crowded exits at the rear. Mark and Steve sat on the floor and stared at each other in total shock and disbelief... or was it now total belief?

***

London.
April 6th.

Steve Hansen prepared for his latest video. It was one he was averse to doing given the events of the night before in the BBC studio but it had to be done. The people needed to know the story first-hand from someone who had experienced the event live, and not some other social media commentator relaying second-hand information that they had seen on the national news broadcasts. It was his 'scoop'.

"Afternoon, good people. Well, you've all seen the tragic news, my friends. Six hundred and eighteen dead and many thousands injured after the freak giant hailstorm yesterday in London. Most were at the BBC headquarters where I was doing a show called The Agenda with a load of climate and government big-wigs, all of which are unfortunately no longer with us, as well as dozens of audience members and the presenter, Ayah Shanise. I barely escaped, along with the author Mark Mason, purely by luck it seems, maybe it was by design? I don't really know for sure. Mark actually pushed me to the floor of the studio and saved my life. Massive thanks to him for that. Of course condolences go out to the victims and their families but it does confirm that the prediction from 'Mother Earth' was right - ice in summer, although technically we're still in spring but after that heatwave, who knows anymore? The sight of that giant frozen block crashing through the studio roof is something I never want to experience again - ever! Considering that there were several floors above the studio probably gives you an idea of the sheer force and weight of the thing. These emails signing themselves 'Mother Earth' really have to be taken seriously now, I think, not just by me, but by everyone else too. Who or what is sending them? I don't know. They are certainly more effective than some youthful, university brainwashed, middle class idiots blocking motorways, aren't they? It was definitely the most frightening experience of my life last night. So where do we go from here, good people? I suppose we wait for another

email to mysteriously arrive. Maybe the governments around the world will take notice now... and not just ours. So, painful as it is to replay what happened last night, I have to tell my story. Basically, in my opinion, I was on the programme to be ridiculed and for the BBC to make fun of the warnings I'd received. Light entertainment for the brain-dead masses, as usual. I was there to be debunked, laughed at for my views. Luckily there was some support from the writer, but mainly the rest of the panel and the presenter were a little hostile judging from the comments I got pre-show. I don't think many are laughing now, are they? Anyway, 'Mother Earth' predicted ice in summer. Very rare in itself, of course, but the timing and location was interesting. Was there a more appropriate time for this latest phenomenon than during a programme designed to shift the blame and to make fun of me and the claim of the mystery emails sent to me? Probably not, to be honest, although the massive loss of life is regrettable, of course. And don't forget the tragic incident in Cornwall the day before. 'Mother Earth' warned me of that too. Judging from the comments on the latest video I put out, the public, on the whole, believe there is someone or something trying to warn us all. Yes, there have been a few calling it all a hoax, whether on my part or perpetrated by this 'Mother Earth'. I can only say that there never was any possibility of a hoax from this channel, and never will be, and I think that any other accusations are now obsolete, don't you think? This thing is very real. These events are terrifyingly real. I suppose we now have to wait until either there is another email warning us of a future disaster or the governments of the world, and not just a few of them, ALL of them, decide to work together and announce effective measures to combat the potential destruction of the planet. Our planet. Then maybe these emails and, more importantly, these disasters will stop. We'll have to wait and see, won't we? As you've just seen, no jokes from me today. It's certainly not the time for humour. I'll catch you all tomorrow when, hopefully, I'll be back to my best and continue to make fun of those you love to hate and I'd rather not have to talk about yet another massive loss of life. Thanks for watching and don't forget to like the video and subscribe if you are not a regular viewer. Hit that bell icon too for notifications of all my new content and, please, look after yourselves, good people."

"That was great, Steve," said Pete. "I'll get that through post prod as soon as I can and get it uploaded to the platform. By the way, forgot to tell you. I set you up on Rumble as well, probably a bit less woke and restrictive than Youtube and definitely the sort of audience we want."

"Thanks Pete. That was probably the hardest video I've had to make so far. I didn't want to mention the scenes of confusion afterwards. The headless chickens at the BBC panicking and the awful crush at the exits that killed more than the bloody chunks of ice. Christ - what a total mess, all that blood, Pete. So unnecessary, mate."

"Let me get this video sorted and we'll go for a drink, get everything off your chest. Talk it through, Steve," said Pete, very concerned for the mental health of his best friend. Steve looked totally drained by the experience. It hadn't done Pete much good either, watching it all live on TV at home with his wife and sister in law.

Kings Langley, Hertfordshire.
April 9th.

Mrs. Jepson and her daughter, Shirley, were sitting in the back garden of the shabby sixties council house. They were celebrating getting Mrs. Jepson's eldest son, Dan, evicted after concocting a fake crime and having him arrested by the police. They both felt very smug as they sat in rusty garden chairs around a dirty algae covered glass table in the middle of an unkempt lawn while drinking cheap white wine from Aldi. The daughter always boasted about how much money she had but always bought the cheapest wine she could find. But then again, she was pretty cheap herself. Always had been. A council estate slapper who tried to talk with a posh accent, but everyone knew exactly what she was.

"I finally got rid of him for you," said Shirley gleefully, "It took a few years to get shot of that parasite, but I did it."

"I wonder what he's doing now," replied Mrs Jepson with an obvious fake concern, a month after her son was evicted, but not bothering to call and check like most mothers would. In her own mind she had a reason for hating her own son. Or ex-son now as he had sent her a letter of emancipation and legally cutting off all contact after she had shown no apparent interest in his wellbeing. Not even to her friends.

"Who cares?" said the psychopathic daughter, "I hope he's freezing on a park bench or has hung himself."

The pair had held a grudge against Dan ever since he was 10 years old and his dad wanted a divorce from his mum. He wanted to go and live with his dad to stop his old man from getting lonely. He thought it would be a nice thing to do. Dan cared about people. Animals too. But his dad found out he had stomach cancer shortly afterwards so he didn't leave after all. He had died mercifully quickly six months later but the hate for Dan from the rest of his family was still there, it festered for decades. His sister started off telling lies about him. He'd lost countless friends without even knowing why. No one would even tell him. At first the hate towards him from his family didn't bother him that much, he was content to plod along, minding his own business and causing no drama for anyone while Mrs. Jepson's daughter bullied everyone around her, including her own mother, which made their closeness seem very strange, and she barely escaped an attempted manslaughter charge when she was fifteen, beating up a young girl and throwing her in the local canal. She was suspended from school for two weeks for that. Being sacked for theft from two jobs and another one for racist bullying really summed up her warped, sick character. The younger son, Kyle, was no better - an alcoholic, violent thug who was once jailed for drink-driving. Dan always wondered if he'd got more love and respect if he'd actually broken the law - it seemed to work for the other two. His only real crime was taking a few sweets from the Pick n' Mix in Woolworths when he was about twelve. Something he still felt guilty about.

Over the years the psychological abuse got even worse. "You should be in an orphanage, you're not wanted, you shouldn't be here, you are a parasite, do everyone a favour and kill yourself." Every word a grain of sand that eventually built itself into a desert for him as far as his family was concerned. He felt he'd never been loved, didn't know how to love in return. He hadn't received one kind word from his mother for as long as he could remember. She even lied about him to her friends saying he was useless, and didn't do anything for her, wasn't to be trusted and never paid her any money for his keep, despite him doing the shopping, driving her to appointments and providing thousands of pounds worth of technical help on her computer, mainly getting rid of viruses she'd downloaded after opening emails promising free money. He realised he couldn't fix stupid... or greed.

After the fake crime report, Dan spent twenty-two hours in a police cell before he was released with a 'No Further Action' - all charges dropped because of no evidence, but was told by the police that Mrs Jepson didn't want him back at the house, no doubt bullied to do so by the vindictive daughter. He was prevented from retrieving any of his property from his bedroom apart from once in the presence of a WPC who stood over him as he grabbed a few clothes, all put in a battered travel case. Everything else was taken out by the brother and his two sons and put in two sheds but a lot of items went missing - either thrown away or stolen. The worst was a hard drive containing thousands of photos of places Dan had visited in the UK and a trip to the US including a helicopter trip over Niagara Falls, things that could never be replaced. One hard drive had all Dan's bank details on it, statements, copies of letters and pin numbers. About two weeks after the eviction he was locked out of his banking app and the bank's website so had to call them and was told his access had been suspended because someone had repeatedly tried to reset his password but failed on the memorable word security. He got it all sorted out quite quickly and the bank assured him they would investigate the failed hacking attempt.

Every cloud has a silver lining, though. Dan eventually got a flat from the council and cut all ties with his ex-family and was finally happy for the first time in nearly fifty years. Dan truly believed in Karma and knew he would be rewarded in some way for trying to be a decent bloke all those years. He owed a lot to the few friends who supported him and helped him and really kept him going in the first few weeks of the four months living in a homeless hostel. They collected and donated items for the new flat. Essential things like a microwave, toaster, kettle, bedding, etc. He really was grateful to them all. The irony was that a few of them had been friends of his ex-mother and who now wanted nothing to do with her, finally realising that her eccentricities were really her being heartless towards everyone... and not just Dan. All Dan wanted was to be left alone by the ex-family. Their vindictiveness was obviously an obsession. His friends meant everything to him now.

Mrs. Jepson felt a faint tremble beneath her feet and the crazy, coke-head daughter watched her third glass of cheap wine vibrate and move slowly towards the edge of the table before toppling off onto the long, unkempt grass. They looked at each other, both very confused, just before a ten foot radius of earth around them sank into the ground with the speed of a train.

Thirty feet below the surface they lay tangled amongst the rusty garden chairs and were groaning loudly, Mrs. Jepson had broken her hip and the daughter had broken a leg and arm when she had landed and when they realised they could not get up or out of the hole (they had metaphorically dug for themselves?) they wailed loudly. The blue cloudless sky dominated their view above the perfectly round circumference of the deep shaft. Wisps of fine dry earth periodically fell from the sides of the yawning pit. They were worried the sides of the shaft were going to collapse in on them but then something far worse happened.

Millions of red ants emerged from the sides of the pit, twin antennae twitching erratically, the ants initially looking like tiny crimson specks on the walls to the two women down below. Within seconds every inch of the walls around them were a seething, undulating carpet of red and it was getting closer to them by the second. Panic set in and neighbours could hear the screams but weren't concerned about the two pariahs of the community. Word had got around about what they had done to Dan. Mrs. Jepson had lost all the friends she had made in the street over the past fifty-six years in just a few days, once the truth was known.

The ants slowly moved lower and lower until they reached the two women. They tentatively crawled over them, nipping away at flabby white flesh, entering open mouths no longer able to scream through shock. Nostrils and ears were quickly clogged with the little red creatures. The two of them were being eaten from inside as well as the saggy cold flesh on the outside. The ants discovered the pair of them were rotten to the core but still fed in a frenzy. The bloated creatures then disappeared back into the walls of the pit again, leaving no trace that they were ever there.

The next day, Paul, the window cleaner, turned up and saw the strange round hole in the back garden and went to investigate. He peered over the edge and saw two skeletons lying at the bottom of the pit thirty feet below and pointlessly called for an ambulance. There was no sympathy from the neighbours or the ex-friends.

Dan was informed of the strange deaths the next day and was even questioned during the police investigation, a possible revenge attack was mooted by them. But as soon as the post mortem results were in he was released. The report showed massive amounts of formic acid on the two skeletons. Neither Dan nor his good friends felt any sympathy for the vindictive pair though. None felt any guilt for feeling that way either.

Karma really is a bitch.

There were many more instances of sinkholes all over the UK that day. Whole families gone, half the players in a charity cricket match, including a few 'celebrities' in another incident and more than one hundred gone during an open air rock concert. All discovered to have been devoured by the red ants. Possibly, collectively, the most gruesome disaster the country had ever seen... so far. Almost anything was possible now.

Westminster, London.
April 12th.

"Ants of all things!" screamed the Prime Minister. "Bloody ants!"

"I've never known anything like it, Prime Minister," replied the environmental advisor, Martin Fenis-Wilkie. "Of course ants can be very dangerous and destructive in large swarms like in South America but not here in this country. They are, or should be, fairly harmless and have only really affected crops in the past. I don't think we've ever had death by ants in our entire history."

"So what can we do to prevent any further attacks, Martin?" asked the Prime Minister, still fuming.

"We're still monitoring the situation but to be honest none of the other disasters have been repeated so far, so I think we shouldn't really waste too many resources on this being replicated, Sir," said the advisor. "And, of course, we can't predict what will happen next, it's virtually impossible, it's all been very random so far."

"So we just sit here with our fingers up our arses, do we? I want answers, Martin! I need bloody answers! Lives are at stake."

"I know you do, Sir. We all do, but there is just no way to predict what will happen... or even where."

"I know. You are right, Martin. I feel so helpless at the moment. At least with a terrorist threat we know who and why, but with these disasters... so unpredictable."

"What about this 'Mother Earth' theory which has been peddled about by the fringe media, Sir? Do you have any thoughts on that?"

"It all seems a bit ludicrous to me. That something supernatural can be causing all this mayhem. Doesn't make sense. But there have been some warnings and these predictions, prophesies, threats, call them what you will, have all happened. Obviously we are doing all we can to trace those emails sent to this Hansen chap. I'm not convinced he's entirely innocent though, why him? At first I thought it was all a hoax, a sick publicity stunt to take advantage of real natural disasters but now... I have no bloody idea, Martin. The devastation is obviously very real so we have to look at all the possibilities, however strange, and one of those is that this 'Mother Earth' is a real threat. Not only to this country but potentially to the whole world. My money is still on a terrorist group though, and that is where most of our resources will be looking at for the moment."

"What if it really is 'Mother Earth' doing this? Some kind of real entity causing these events to show us all that we are heading towards the end of life on this planet as we know it? I know it sounds a bit far-fetched but every scientist in the world will admit there are things and forces that we still don't fully understand and probably never will. Maybe there is some sort of superior being safeguarding the world? Maybe this is what people have referred to as 'God' all these thousands of years? Not an entity who is there for man in times of crisis but is only there for the planet."

"Some people do believe in some sort of planetary spirit, they call it Gaia, but right now we're desperate for an answer, Martin, any answer at all, Gaia or not," said the Prime Minister. "Then, perhaps, we'll have a solution to this utter madness. And then do our best to try and reverse things."

London.
April 17th.

"*Welcome to a rare live broadcast on this channel, good people,*" *said Steve Hansen, pausing for a few seconds now and again to wait for more viewers to jump onto the stream.*

"*I hope everyone is doing okay and surviving the day to day hassles and dramas we have to put up with. Let's thank a few superfans while we wait for any latecomers. Dee49 asks if I'm single. Well, Dee, thanks for the donation. Maybe I can use that fiver to buy you a Big Mac meal, heh, heh. Only joking, sweetie. To be honest with the amount of time I spend with Pete we may as well be married and the good thing is he doesn't buy more new shoes every weekend like the ex-wife.*

"*PatrickMcGrath365 says I should do more live streams just to show how ignorant I am. Thanks Patrick. You are entitled to your opinion and its cost you a couple of quid of your hard earned wages. I wish I had a stress free job like stacking shelves at Aldi like you, cheers mate.*

"*Lesley/Leslie asks if I should promote Trans rights a bit more on the show. Well, Lesley/Leslie, If I did that I'd have to promote every single minority equally and if I devoted more time to one over all the others I'd be called a lot of nasty names and probably get cancelled or even stalked so I try to treat everyone the same and not promote any division between all you good people. I really only have the time to stick to current events and have my say and let other people in the spotlight spew their hate. That's the job of the mainstream media, as well as spreading fear, in my opinion so we'll leave it all to them, Okay? This channel is more about making fun of some people and having a good laugh at their expense. Thanks for the generous superfan donation though, and hope that answers your question.*

"*SaveThePlanet247 wonders if the Mother Earth emails are real and if 'she' is really controlling things and causing all these disasters. Well, thanks, SaveThePlanet247. At first I thought it was a complete hoax as the original email from 'Mother Earth' did come to me on April Fools Day, but over the last few weeks there have been more and more things happening, not just in the UK but all over Europe and this person or entity, or whatever they are, does predict a lot of them correctly so I suppose we really need to keep an open mind, don't we? Is it all real or just coincidence? I don't really know for sure and, as you can probably tell, I still have my doubts. It's a bit scary to think that someone has all that power to make these events happen and what they could actually be capable of. Whoever or whatever they are, it does needs to stop."*

Just then the room began to shake and the microphone on its boom swung towards the face of Steve Hansen and he tried to duck to avoid it but it caught the top of his head, carving a deep gash. Blood flowed into his eyes and down his face and then covered the untidy desk. His white mouse and keyboard now had bloody crimson splashes like a bad expressionist painting. Steve looked around in shock and saw Pete trying to keep the camera on the host, trying not to panic too much himself.

The live comments box displayed on the PCs and phones of the audience suddenly went mad.

James Smith: "WTF? What's happening?"

MerryMandy: "You OK, Steve?"

Bobby Dazzler 69: "Is that a fucking earthquake there, mate?"

PussyFace1: "I didn't feel anything and I'm not too far away, everyone."

SpandexDude: "Is everyone okay there, man?"

Mother Earth: "People need to take heed, Mr. Hansen. Never doubt me ever again."

Steve gathered himself and stared into the camera lens looking like Carrie at the end of the Prom - all wide eyed, confused and covered in blood. Unfortunately it was his own and not pig's blood.

"I'm not too sure what has happened, everyone. I think it's time we ended this stream for today and get myself and the place cleaned up a bit. I hope everyone out there is safe and well and I'll try to get back to you all a bit later for an update. Looks like I may be off to hospital. I hope it's not a twelve hour wait."

Pete stopped the camera recording and looked outside the window. Everything seemed absolutely normal. People were going about their day's business, totally oblivious to what had happened two floors above them. He stared at Steve with incredulity - the "earthquake" had apparently only been felt in the studio.

Deal, Kent.
April 19th.

Neville Hall, senior sports master at St. Jude's school in the centre of Deal, led the excited boys onto the football field. It was a sunny Tuesday afternoon and it was the last period of the day. The weather had been fine for about a week so the pitch was pretty dry even after being watered almost every day since the recent heatwave. Hall was pleased it wasn't muddy because these little eleven-year-old buggers made a right mess of the showers and changing room and he felt a bit sorry for the school caretaker, Mr. Tripp, having to clean all that mud up, sometimes even a lot of toilet paper too if the boys got a bit rowdy, which they usually did, especially after the last period when they could all rush off home and not be held accountable for any mess and leaving everything for poor old Mr. Tripp to sort out.

"Come on you lazy lot, organise yourself into two teams. No, Jarvis! On the other team please, let's make things a bit fairer. I don't want *all* you better lads on the same team. I want a nice even game this time. Goodman! Stop that! Do it at home if you have to do it at all!"

The two teams were finally picked, he blew the whistle for the start of the practice game - twenty minutes each way. He'd been quite impressed with young Jarvis over the last few weeks. The boy was growing at a rapid rate and would probably hit six feet in a year or so. He wouldn't be surprised if the lad got a trial at one of the local clubs, maybe even at one of the big clubs in London. Jarvis was a tricky winger with plenty of pace and had the good looks to be very media and sponsor friendly if he made it in the professional game. But that was a long way off. For now he just wanted the boy to enjoy himself with no pressure, although he knew there would be scouts in attendance if his boys got to the cup final at the end of May. Just three more wins and they were there. The ground at Folkestone wasn't Wembley, but it may be the only chance to win a trophy for most of these lads.

Hall had been a sports master at the school for nearly twenty years and had seen a lot of kids come and go but knew Jarvis was head and shoulders above any kid he'd seen there. Not only a good footballer but was good at rugby too and would do well at athletics next term. Strong and full of speed. He'd make a great sprinter, as well as excel in the long jump.

Julian Whitton wasn't very good at football so he was usually stuck in goal. The ball was at the other end of the pitch so he took that opportunity to try and tie his loose boot lace with his gloved hands. As he knelt down he started to feel a bit strange then rolled over onto his back.

"Whitton, stop playing the goat, boy!" shouted Hall from the other end of the pitch. "Get up, lad. Now!"

Whitton lay where he was as Hall jogged towards him. "Whitton! I'm starting to lose my patience, lad. Get up or its detention for you!... Whit-," He could see something was obviously wrong with the youngster. The boy wasn't messing around for once.

As he crouched down to see what was wrong, he too keeled over and lay on top of the boy. The rest of the boys started to laugh and then ran over to see what had happened and as they stood bending over around the stricken duo, wondering what was occurring, started to collapse themselves. All except the tall Jarvis who, seeing all his friends fall to the ground, sprinted for the school office to get some help.

Over an hour later, two men in Hazmat suits from Environmental Services were on the field taking readings on their portable machines, stepping over the small bodies whose faces were tinged a light blue. They eventually returned to the school yard, which was situated on a bank a good twenty feet above the football field a hundred yards away in a slight valley. They made their report to the senior officers present from the police and fire service.

"Carbon monoxide, Sir," said Alan Marks, the more experienced of the two testing the air around the bodies.

"Where did it come from, Marks?" asked Potter, the police superintendent, standing there in his pristine uniform just in case the media arrived.

"It seems to have seeped up from the ground near the far goal. Just a small area, maybe a radius of around fifteen yards but as you can see, the teacher and the boys all flocked to the same area. That lad was saved by his height," nodding towards Jarvis, who was shivering with a blanket over his shoulders, being comforted by a couple of female admin staff from the school. He was obviously overcome by shock and sadness for the loss of his friends.

"So what's the best course of action, Marks," asked the fire officer.

"Well, the gas seems to have pretty much dissipated already, Sir," replied Marks. "Just a very small trace of it left an inch or two above ground and looks like its rapidly seeping back into the earth. It's strange. Of course we'll cordon that area off and test some more over the next few days. We'll also run the ground penetrating radar over the whole area to try and determine just where the pocket of gas is located and then we can use chemicals to neutralise it."

"So it's safe enough to retrieve the bodies now?" asked Potter.

"Pretty safe, although I'd advise wearing basic breathing apparatus just in case, but there shouldn't be a problem now. The level of gas has reduced from possibly just over five feet to a couple of inches in around an hour and a half and at that rate by the time the paramedics get the victims out of the area it should have totally gone back underground. We'll be back tomorrow with the GPR and we'll get the cordon tapes up after the last of those poor kids are removed."

In all, twenty-one boys and the forty-five year old Hall died at St. Jude's that afternoon. Another tragedy for the whole country to mourn. The mainstream media, always keen on a tragedy, especially involving children, were all over the story within a couple of hours. Experts were interviewed, but were at a loss as to why the gas level rose and then receded so quickly. Pointless interviewing them, but they were happy to get their fifteen minutes of fame.

***

The next day Marks and his assistant arrived with the GPR kit. They staked and taped the ground near the goal into a grid and patiently went to work, watched by a few school staff who had come in even though they had been given the opportunity to stay away. All the remaining children had been given the day off which, of course, they took. Two hours later Marks packed the gear up and then went to find the headmaster, Nigel Hockey. He found him in his office, a neat and tidy little enclave which Hockey could relax in. The headmaster offered a seat in a brown cloth covered chair to Marks who was grateful he was in his normal blue boiler suit instead of the bulky white and yellow Hazmat gear he was wearing the previous day.

"So, what did you find? I hope we won't have to dig up the sports field to get rid of this gas, Mr. Marks."

"No, there's no need for that. Our radar didn't pick up any pockets of gas at all which was very strange considering what happened yesterday. To be honest I'm stumped, Mr. Hockey. It's quite bizarre to be honest. I've not experienced anything quite like this in almost twenty-two years on the job. It's like the gas rose quickly from nowhere in a concentrated flow onto the field and then seeped back into the ground again after killing the group of boys and the teacher. It's like it had a mind of its own. There is absolutely no trace of it at all now. As far as I can tell the field is safe and there will be no repetition of yesterday's events."

"Extraordinary indeed. I have a fair knowledge of Geology and have never heard of that myself either. I know underground gas pockets are relatively common, especially near coastal areas like this and the gas is siphoned off for safety reasons which is mainly to avoid explosions, but for CO2 to come and go like that is virtually impossible in my limited experience - it didn't even disperse in the air - it just sank again after killing my boys and poor Mr. Hall. We were good friends, you know, we have been for a lot of years. I'm a godparent to his daughter. Christ, I really need to see her," sighed the headmaster. "What a complete mess. I feel for all the parents of the boys too, obviously, but Caroline Hall is almost like my own daughter. I didn't ring her last night - I just didn't want to intrude, but I will go around and see her today once I have things squared away here. I know all the paperwork is necessary, but by the time I get to do it for the twenty-first boy I'll need a break for a few days. I'll need to organise a memorial service for everyone next week, or are they called 'vigils' now?"

"I have no idea, Mr. Hockey. Anyway, I need to liaise with the police and fire service again and tell them my findings, or lack of, to be more accurate. Please let me know when the memorial is - I'd like to attend."

"Thank you, Mr. Marks, I'll let you know," sighed Hockey.

Marks shook the sweaty, chubby hand of the headmaster and exited the cosy office into the main admin building, said goodbye to the remaining staff, and joined his assistant in the van.

Hockey tried to continue with the paperwork relating to the deaths of his boys and after a few minutes held his head in his hands and wept uncontrollably. *Why my school? WHY?* He thought.

London.
July 2nd.

Steve Hansen was preparing for his next broadcast. He sat there with a bandage on his forehead covering the eight stitches holding together the gaping wound caused by the swinging microphone during the localised 'earthquake'. It seemed incredible that only he and Pete had felt it and no one else in the immediate area. He had watched the video of his livestream several times and it obviously had happened the way he remembered it. And the viewers saw the earthquake too judging by the messages. Lots of concern for his safety from the loyal fans but one message stood out over all the others:

Mother Earth: "People need to take heed, Mr. Hansen."

It sent chills up and down his spine.

He was now a believer. One hundred and ten percent, and that scared him. Mother Earth had specifically targeted him. Made an example of him exactly at the point when he said he still doubted the phenomena.

Just then his email software alerted him with a beep. He clicked on the icon at the bottom of the screen and on top of the usual spam there was one with the heading; **Do you believe now?** As usual, there was nothing in the From: column.

He hesitated for several seconds, maybe even close to a minute, thoughts racing through his head and a memory of the mike boom swinging towards his head. Then he opened the email.

Mr. Hansen,

I'm hoping you have taken the hint and now believe what I am capable of. You do need to convince your audience that I am real and I am responsible for the incidents that have taken place over the last few months. You have to believe that I bear no ill will against any individuals but the whole population of this country and many other countries too. Things

have gone too far and even with a concerted effort by every country on the planet it will be difficult to restore the harmony with Nature we once had, but we must salvage what we can and we have to do it NOW! You do have to get the word out to everyone to urgently change their ways or this world WILL become inhabitable for them. The Earth will always survive and adapt but there will be no humans left to pollute it further the way things are developing. Make them listen, Mr. Hansen. In a few days there will be an event in the West of Europe. That is the only warning I'll give you. Things are in motion and cannot be stopped at this late stage. Keep watching your news channels because I will do whatever it takes to convince everyone that I am the one in control now and will do ANYTHING to stop the disgusting desecration of our world.

Mother Earth.

Steve clicked on 'Reply'. He had so many questions for this 'Mother Earth', they were racing through his head and he needed answers, something he could pass on to the government.

A box popped up on his screen saying:

*PRIVATE DOMAIN. **You cannot contact this mailbox.***

"Shit!" Steve muttered under his breath. "Shit, shit, shit."

Vera looked at the alert on her computer which told her that someone, obviously Steve Hansen, had tried to reply to the email she'd sent. As she worked for the Security Services she knew a few tricks to stop anyone tracking her. She had worked at one of the many surveillance sub-stations dotted around the country over the years, offshoots of GCHQ. She monitored phone calls and text messages which flagged up key words like 'bomb', 'attack', 'Downing Street', and the like. Most people didn't realise that when they called their bank the voice recognition software to direct them to the right person or service was developed by GCHQ in the Eighties and, now obsolete, was sold on to companies to generate money for bigger and better projects. People thought they knew what sort of technology these domestic spies had but whatever they imagined they were twenty years out of date. Vera knew that if a flagged call or text was deemed credible then there would be action within minutes.

Obviously most arrests were kept secret under the D-Notice which meant there would be a media ban on all reporting of the operation. The general public really had no idea how many terrorist plots were foiled in Britain every year. They wouldn't moan about how much tax they paid if they did. She loved her job. It made her feel vital to the security of the country. She had no friends at all. Either at work or in her private life and it had been like that since her school days. It didn't bother her. She had her interests and now she had her quest to save the planet. What could be more important?

She had been recruited straight from Cambridge University. She had always shown well above average analytical skills and a high intelligence. Vera had been twenty-two at the time and was looking to get into a career in research. She was always interested in gaining knowledge and did very well in school despite the bullies picking on her year after year. All were dealt with one way or another but not in the way Karen Mills was. Nothing too obvious again. A couple of them were hit by cars crossing a busy road against their will, one drowned in the school swimming pool. The most satisfying one was Kelly Martin, a nasty little girl from a nasty family. She was forced to eat Deadly Nightshade berries, lots of them. Vera made it look like she was eating the berries to show off to her friends and prove how tough she was, but it was really Vera controlling her actions, Kelly's behaviour and especially what she had said to her friends. It took several days for Kelly to die horribly. She started to get headaches and a bad rash, then awful hallucinations and finally convulsions, which eventually killed her. Vera particularly enjoyed Kelly's painful death. All these bullies fully deserved what they had got and the best part was no one ever suspected Vera of anything. She was always in the area. She like to watch. She was never suspected of anything although she had been questioned a couple of times as a witness.

Vera thought about Gerald again. He certainly deserved what happened to him too.

London.

July 3rd.

Steve Hansen waited patiently to be called into the office in Downing Street. He had been shocked into wakefulness by the uniformed police knocking on his door at 7:30 that morning and his first reaction was obviously what he'd done. His foggy mind racing through the possibilities, dismissing most.

"Good morning Mr. Hansen, would you mind coming with us, Sir?" asked the one with sergeant's stripes on his sleeve.

Sir? Steve thought. *That's a good sign, at least they haven't battered the door down and got me in handcuffs yet.*

"What's this all about, sergeant?" he asked.

"You've been summoned by a VIP, Sir. It will all be explained when you get there, Sir," said the sergeant.

"A VIP? Bloody hell, they must be important for you to ask nicely," smirked Steve, his mistrust of the police shining through. "Give me a few minutes to shower and dress, will you?"

"Of course, Sir. Do you mind if we wait inside?"

"Fine," replied Steve, who quickly showered and then dressed in his bedroom while the two coppers waited patiently on the sofa in the living room. He'd had his stitches removed from his forehead the previous day and his head was still a little sore but luckily there would be no real scar from the incident with the microphone during his own personal earthquake courtesy of Mother Earth.

He re-entered the living room and noticed the two policemen drinking mugs of tea. *Cheeky buggers!* He thought.

"Hope you don't mind, Sir," grinned the sergeant.

"Not at all," replied Steve, grudgingly.

The drive only took forty minutes through the centre of London. Steve soon recognised the gates of Downing Street as they approached.

"Jesus, I suppose they really are a VIP," remarked Steve as the gates were opened by another couple of young uniformed coppers who then waved the car through.

"We'll just get you signed in and then you'll have to wait in the reception area until you are called, Mr. Hansen."

Steve stood at the large mahogany desk looking longingly at a pretty young lady with 'Zoe Baxter' on her security name badge seated behind it tapping at a computer keyboard. He thought she was gorgeous but he was way out of her league. Probably engaged to someone called Tarquin whose mummy and daddy owned half of Surrey. A right cracker though, he thought. Posh totty at it's very best.

"Mr. Steven Hansen? I have your details up on the screen. Can you confirm your date of birth, National Insurance number and address for me please?"

Steve smiled at her and gave her the requested information and then winked when he asked her if she needed his inside leg measurement too.

"We already have that, Mr. Hansen," she smiled. "Please take a seat over there." She pointed to a row of grey seats against the far wall of the reception area.

Steve wondered if she was joking about his measurements or not. Was it really as much of a police and surveillance state some of his subscribers keep telling him in the video comments? He wouldn't be surprised now.

After a wait of nearly thirty minutes a tall man in a very dark, well-tailored suit approached Steve and he was told that the PM was ready to see him. He followed the man up a long semi-spiral staircase, trying to keep up and looking at the portraits of previous Prime Ministers on the wall. He was reminded of a few unsavoury characters who had been in charge over the years and that picture of dear old Maggie Thatcher almost gave him the shivers. He was surprised the alleged kiddie fiddler was still there but taking it down would almost certainly be an admission of his guilt, he supposed. Whatever happened to that investigation into child abuse in Westminster that was supposed to be happening? Probably swept under the carpet yet again. They only seemed to be exposed after they were dead a few years. A bit like the BBC. He was then shown into a small, but cosy room, the cosiness almost ruined by the large bank of TV screens opposite the desk. Robert Garland, the Prime Minister, was there sitting behind a desk while another man in a dark suit, presumably some kind of personal protection, sat on a chair in the corner looking slightly menacingly at Steve.

"Sit down, Hansen," said Garland. He wasn't wearing his usual politician's 'I want your vote' smile. He looked rather angrily at Steve. He sat on a seat on the other side of the large desk Garland as instructed. The desk looked ancient, teak maybe? "Thank you, Adams, you can wait outside," Garland said to the man who had escorted Steve up the stairs.

Steve felt nervous, wondering what this was all about.

"I'll get straight to the point, Hansen. Why you?"

Steve immediately grasped why he was there. "Ah, you mean this Mother Earth? I have no idea. She said it was because I had an audience. She probably meant they were easily influenced I suppose, easily led."

"I see," replied Garland, disappointed.

"I'm surprised I wasn't suspected of causing all the events," said Steve.

"Oh, believe me, you were, Hansen. At first anyway. You've been very closely monitored over the last couple of weeks and your close call at the BBC pretty much confirmed you weren't involved. We've also ruled out a hoax on your part. We now believe this Mother Earth is quite real and responsible for these disasters. We don't know how yet, but we're hopeful and have one or two ideas soon."

"Good to hear," smiled Steve. So who do you think is behind it all? My money is on the Chinese. Some advanced weapon of some kind?"

"The Chinese have been ruled out. So have the Russians and North Koreans," replied Garland. "Middle East rogue states too... you know the ones, I'm sure."

"Surely not aliens, then?" laughed Steve.

"We're keeping an open mind, Hansen, but I highly doubt it's extra-terrestrial. Suffice to say that whoever, or whatever, is responsible, they will be tracked down and dealt with severely. And that is where I demand your assistance."

"Demand?" said Steve, feeling like he was being railroaded into something. He didn't like to be pushed around - not even by the bloody Prime Minister. And he certainly didn't like this knob using just his surname all the time. Posh dickhead.

"Let me put it this way. Refusing to help would not be a good idea on your part. For a start I can shut you down immediately. Stop you broadcasting for good, as well as get you remanded in custody for months on end for any number of crimes, real or imagined," Garland grinned slyly. "No, you won't turn me down, I'm assuming, Hansen."

"Well, if you put it that way I really have no choice. Reminds me why I voted for the other lot at the last election." Steve enjoyed that counter punch as he knew he was on the ropes and there was no real escape. "What do you want me to do?"

"One of our security agencies, I won't say which one, will visit your office later today to install monitoring software on your existing equipment. Of course, they could have done that without your permission or even knowledge. They are very good at what they do, but for legal reasons, say, if this person or organisation ever does get to court, then getting you to sign a document giving your permission would solve any problems later," said Garland. "We really can't afford to get the case thrown out of court on a technicality, can we?"

"Sounds fair enough. My tech guy will have to be told, of course," said Steve. "I'm sure you don't want him finding something fishy during his daily virus check and then deleting it."

"Oh, their software would never be detected during a virus check and even if it was it can't be deleted without a security key, anyway. And that key is several dozen characters long and would take years to break, if ever. But your man will be pretty much informed of what the security bods are installing," Garland conceded.

"Well, let's hope your fancy bit of kit works and it traces those buggers responsible."

"I'm confident it will, Hansen," said Garland, although he looked far from convinced.

"Of course, one solution would be to actually give in to this Mother Earth's demands," Steve pointed out. It already seems to half the country that the proposed measures have so far been empty promises and even higher taxes for all of us. Maybe actually doing something for once may appease whoever is causing this, or at least give you a bit of breathing space, possibly delay more events too."

"I can assure you that all the major world leaders have already been in a remote conference and plans are being put in place all around the world. Announcements will be made soon enough, once things have been organised," replied Garland.

"The majority would think that all this could have been prevented if you'd all acted years ago. And kept all those promises," said Steve, knowing he'd hit a nerve with the Prime Minister. "Too little, too late, as usual. Still, we have to keep the toffs in Westminster in caviar and thirty year old single malt, don't we?" He enjoyed that quip.

"That will be enough, Hansen. You can go now. Adams will show you out and the police car is ready to take you home again." The silent protection man rose to his feet, opened the door and wordlessly waved Adams in, who led Steve to the back entrance of 10 Downing Street where the police car was waiting. Steve asked to be taken to his office instead of home. He needed to call Pete from his mobile while in the car to get him in the office as soon as possible. They needed a serious talk about all this - especially about that bloody spyware. Pete was the tech expert. Steve was largely ignorant about all that stuff. He knew Pete would be furious.

Pete arrived at the office about twenty-five minutes after Steve and immediately put the kettle on. Steve filled Pete in on the events of the morning and said the security people would be there that afternoon and they would hopefully be done before the next broadcast planned for around six pm. Pete was absolutely fuming at first, but Steve pointed out that they had no choice in the matter. It was either co-operate with them or risk being shut down, maybe for good. Garland had made that 'perfectly clear' which happened to be one of the PM's ready catch-phrases when trying to evade a straight answer to something. Steve also told Pete that if they had a hand in catching the nutter, or nutters, then the publicity would be great for the channel, maybe even lead to TV or something. Pete was reluctantly placated enough to accept things. He still wasn't happy about someone fiddling with his tech but finally realised they really did have no choice.

"Looks like the removal of those stitches went well, mate. I'll stop the Harry Potter jokes now."

"About time, you dick," smiled Steve. "If it didn't muffle my eloquent voice I'd wrap the mike in foam rubber so I don't suffer the same fate again. Although

I'm sure Mother Earth, if they were responsible for our personal tremor, would find something else to hit us with. Or technically, hit me with!"

"Let's try our best to avoid anything like that again, eh?" said Pete as he filled the kettle again.

***

It was dead on 3pm when two large men in suits arrived at the office, both carrying large brushed metal cases with combination locks. Steve let them in while Pete sat on the sofa staring at them suspiciously, trying to stay calm but worried about his expensive kit. It didn't take very long for them to install the spy software onto the main PC. They explained to Steve that all incoming calls, texts and emails could be tracked to the sender, without fail, and the next time that Mother Earth contacted him by any means they would be able to trace them to wherever they were, whatever country they were in. They made both Steve and Pete sign a form stating their permission to use the tracking software. Steve told them he hoped it worked and they could put an end to not only the disasters but his own personal involvement with the perpetrators. They were uninterested in Steve's thoughts or even concerned. They made that very obvious with their attitudes. The two men left less than twenty minutes after they had arrived, confident that they would soon have this insanity finally at an end.

"I still don't like it, Steve," said Pete, trying and failing to get into the protected folder mocking him from the desktop screen of his PC. "I've never seen encryption anything like this before."

"Probably why they do what they do and you are stuck working with a muppet like me," joked Steve although he himself was far from happy with the situation either. He wondered just what else this spyware was capable of.

"This shit they've put on here had better work... and sharpish, scowled Pete. "You do realise they can spy on us and probably everyone who interacts with us too. This could be some kind of self-replicating virus that could infect the phones and computers of anyone who contacts us, and if that little gem of information ever got out then we'd be screwed and so would the channel."

"Like I told you mate, they have us both by our furry nuts. And Garland was pretty clear about the consequences of refusing and I'm too cute to be raped in prison and so are you." Steve squirmed uncomfortably at the thought.

"How the hell did we get in this shit, Steve?"

"What worries me is why did she, or they, really pick us? The gullible audience thing is just crap, I'll bet. There has to be a better reason and it's bugging the shit out of me... no pun intended," replied Steve, glancing at Pete's main PC. There was something he wasn't getting about all this, it certainly wasn't obvious. "I think we'll delay the next podcast for a couple of days, mate, let's get down the pub, I fancy getting plastered, and luckily the beer supply is almost back to normal. I wouldn't be surprised if that software could pick up our conversations in here too. So for the benefit of anyone listening, your boss, Robert Garland, is a frigging wanker!"

Pete locked the office, put on the alarm and they walked to the pub about a hundred yards down the road. Steve ordered a pint each and also single malt chasers... it had been that sort of day.

Paris.

July 5th.

It was going to be a great day, or so Jean-Michel Clement had hoped. He'd planned this romantic trip for weeks. He was finally going to propose to his long-lime girlfriend, Cecile Dubois. A few days before, he'd suggested a couple of days away from their home in Reims, taking in Paris (surprisingly Cecile had never been to the capital in her entire young life) and then the beautiful Palace of Versailles. What better opportunity to ask her to be his bride than a romantic getaway like this? Jean-Michel and Cecile had lived together for over six years since meeting at an art exhibition in Reims around seven years ago. They adored each other but unusually they had never had a real conversation about any marriage. There were lots of half jokes or one of them subtly avoiding the subject but Jean-Michel thought the time was right to plough headlong into the future. A shared future. He was so nervous.

Jean-Michel and Cecile were in one of the elevators heading for the Eiffel Tower observation platform 276 meters above ground level, feeling a little claustrophobic because stifling heat of early July. It didn't help that a scruffy man in the grey raincoat standing next to them in the elevator smelt a bit off. They finally reached the top and were greeted by bright summer sunshine as the lift doors slowly opened. Jean-Michel moved his sunglasses from the top of his head and placed them over his squinting pale blue eyes. He started to meander around the deck on his own, now getting *very* nervous. What if she said no? It would be a pretty silent trip down again in the elevator and he'd probably punch the smelly guy just for being there in the same elevator. No, he was sure she'd say yes. She just had to. It was destined to be, he knew.

As the sky got slightly darker he thought it was time to finally pluck up the courage to ask her. He didn't really want to do it during one of those summer showers some people actually liked. It really was beginning to get a bit overcast now. Suddenly he became aware of an acute chill on the side of his face. He thought it was probably nerves but the chill slowly increased, he felt it deep in his bones now. Jean-Michel looked up at the fading sunlight from the east. Was that snow he could see? Surely it couldn't be. The first flake landed on his nose, the second on his hand holding the box containing the emerald engagement ring. Everyone else on the observation platform looked up at the sky in amazement, including Cecile. Some were laughing and joking but others looked very nervous, remembering the other disasters that had happened in Western Europe over the last few months and they quickly headed for the elevator, trying not to panic and still retain some dignity.

Jean-Michel stood near the edge of the platform, gripping the cold iron struts, looking out at the gathering clouds. Cecile slowly moved towards him and tried to cuddle him. They were wearing summer clothes and now a severe icy breeze was slicing through them, chilling the pair to the bone. Their minds went numb as the increasing coldness bit into them, an overwhelming lethargy soon overcame the pair. Jean-Michel's hands were stuck to the railing. The same happened to the remaining people on the deck waiting for the lift to return.

As the sub-zero breeze enveloped the whole of Paris, millions stood in the streets, first numbed by the cold and curiosity and then frozen solid as the temperature quickly went down to the minus forties Celsius. Even those indoors weren't saved either. When people realised what was happening and tried to get central heating and furnaces, dormant since April, working in their buildings. It was far too late as hypothermia set in even as they huddled around radiators and heaters in homes and offices all across the freezing city.

At the top of the tower Jean-Michel and Cecile were joined together, not in marriage, but like a pair of chicken breasts tucked away in the back of a freezer drawer. Those who had managed to get into the lifts fared no better as the large metal boxes stopped halfway and they all had died from the intense cold.

Over ninety percent of the population of Paris died that day. The biggest single tragedy in history. The icy breeze strangely did not stretch outside of the city limits. Five million had perished. Another terrible disaster. Another mysterious event of Biblical proportions. The usual climate experts on news channels were stunned and as clueless as ever. They had been banging on about rising temperatures and sea levels and melting polar ice caps for decades and now the opposite had happened. A massive freeze that was strangely contained within the Parisian city limits. The entire population of the planet feared what would come next... and where.

London.
July 6th.

"Hi good people, its Steve Hansen here again. By now you have all heard the tragic and dreadful news from Paris. Millions dead from a mysterious sudden freeze in the city. We really have to do something to end all this. A few days ago I had another email from 'Mother Earth' which had warned of a further disaster in Western Europe. Obviously that is a very large area so impossible to predict where the event would take place. I did try to contact the government to warn them but they were powerless to help but I have been assured that plans were underway to radically change how we, as a planet, deal with worldwide pollution. The thing is that the UK produces less than three percent of this global poisoning so I don't know why we, as a country, have been targeted so much by Mother Earth. So far there have been hardly any incidents in China or India who, collectively, are responsible for about seventy-five percent of air and water pollution. Why the hell not? You have to ask yourself that very serious question, Mother Earth. Why have they been exempt from these disasters so far? Are they the ones causing all these incidents? Is that why they've got off scot-free? Is 'Mother Earth' actually working for a secret Chinese government project? Actually the Prime Minister assured me the Chinese were in the clear when I was hauled in to meet him a few days ago. For those interested, he wanted to know why Mother Earth has been contacting me, of all people. Could this be another form of biological weapon like Covid 19? Is the Western world being targeted to destroy our economies even further? I have to say I believe 'Mother Earth' is real, we saw another example of 'her' powers after what happened during the livestream. The thing with the microphone was not some freak accident, and I'm sure whoever it is believes they are doing all this for the good of everyone. But is it the right way? WE need to convince the governments of every country to act because this person, government, group, agency or even entity or whatever the hell is causing all the disasters needs to know that measures are being taken. That's what the Prime Minister told me anyway. There have been meetings, or rather a digital conference, between the major heads of world governments... or so he says. Personally I don't trust him an inch so we just have to hope all the politicians are telling the truth about seriously trying to tackle the issues we all are

facing. But 'Mother Earth' needs to know that we are all trying to do the right thing, but we need their or her cooperation too. I have to believe that if we are seen to be trying to get everyone together to solve this world pollution these attacks on innocent people, because attacks are clearly what they are, will stop, or at least be paused. I have tried to reply to the emails that 'Mother Earth' has sent me but it's technically not possible, I don't think anyone can, even the boffins at GCHQ, who would have traced her by now if they could. Anyway, at least I haven't been smacked in the face by the microphone today, so things may be looking up for me... and for us all if the world leaders get their arses into gear and solve this pollution problem. But as I've said in the past - ALL nations have to be on board with this initiative and not just the ones taxing their citizens. Rant over, good people. So that is it from me for today, and Pete of course; please stay safe everyone."

"This stuff is really starting to shit me up, mate," said Pete from behind the camera. "Nice one saying GCHQ can't trace her. It may make her a bit complacent, maybe make a mistake through overconfidence and this spy crap on my PC actually works because I don't think for one minute she's careless enough to make it easy for anyone."

"It's really getting to me too, Pete. And there is not a lot we can do about it. Are you getting any close to breaking the encryption of her emails? It would certainly help if we could contact her, get to her before the spies do. It could mean a book deal at the very least. And I'm pretty convinced it is a 'her' now. What self-respecting bloke would call himself 'Mother Earth'? It would be 'Wrath of God' or something more butch, wouldn't it?"

"I'm still trying, Steve. This it some top level shit being used. Advanced Military grade, I reckon," sighed Pete.

"Or supernatural," smiled Steve Hansen grimly.

"Piss off," scowled Pete.

Yellowstone National Park, US (Ranger Station #4).
July 18th.

"Who ate my goddamn Cheetos!" shouted Barry Rockford as the giant of a man angrily stood holding open the cupboard door with a shovel-like hand in the small kitchen area of the Ranger station.

"You should have labelled them, dude," replied Lance Silverman, his Californian accent out of place way out in the hills of Wyoming. "Anyway, it wasn't me, man," said the lithe, blond haired, blue eyed kid from San Diego.

"I bet it was that fat prick, Ellison," scowled Rockford angrily.

"What's the problem now, Barry?" asked Artie Vincenzo, the head ranger. "You woke me from my na...err - I was quietly busy with paperwork."

"The problem is, Art, that some asshat has eaten the giant bag of Cheetos I had in here. It's not like there is a Quick Stop anywhere close so I can go and replace them!" said Rockford, angrily.

"Did you label them, Barry?" asked Vincenzo.

"No, but everyone here knows they are my favourite snack. They should have realised," replied Rockford.

"Maybe it was the squirrels," quipped Lance. "I hear they really go for the BBQ ones."

"Don't start with me, Silverman. It's theft, plain and simple."

"Okay, Barry, it's really no big deal, is it? It's not like your fake Rolex has gone missing. I'll be driving to town later so I'll pick some up for you, what do you say? Crisis over, big guy?"

"Okay, thanks Art," said Rockford, now beginning to realise he'd made an ass of himself by losing his temper over something pretty trivial yet again.

Lance, a typical blond surfer type, lazed in an armchair and scrolled through Twitter on his phone.

"Hey, there's a lot of buzz on this Mother Earth thing, guys. It's so trending right now," he smiled with gleaming white, perfect teeth.

"It's a load of bullcrap, man, just a bunch of natural disasters they are taking the credit for," replied Rockford. "No one can control all these things. Look, we're sitting here right on top of the biggest time bomb in history. If this caldera blows at least half the world is screwed. The ash alone would block out the sun for years, let alone the devastation from the lava and the pyroclastic flow. At least we'd be able to predict an event weeks or months ahead. But relax, we're probably not due another eruption for about two hundred thousand years... plenty of time to get my Cheetos," he laughed, now a lot more chilled out than he was before.

"Still pretty scary, Baz," shivered Lance. "All that raw power right under our damn feet. I wonder if you could surf that pyroclastic wave, man? It would be really rad."

"Far from it. You'd be incinerated in a millisecond, Lance," answered Vincenzo.

"Better than dying of boredom, boss. Nothing much happens around here, does it?" sighed Lance.

"You've only been here a couple of months, just wait until the winter comes, we'll be busy enough tracking down lost hikers and even the odd bear attack just before they hibernate... and of course that Cheeto stealing squirrels," laughed Vincenzo.

Rockford scowled again - he really hated being the butt of any joke. And he really wanted a snack. Goddam Ellison!

***

Lynsey and Jack Bolton were watching the amazing geyser, Old Faithful, on their annual trip to 'somewhere interesting' in the States. Previous years included the Grand Canyon, Hawaii, winter in Alaska, Niagara Falls, Mardi Gras in New Orleans and The Alamo. Jack had been to visit the park before but it was before he married Lynsey. She was absolutely loving this trip though, maybe even more than all the others she's taken with Jack. She was so close to this natural phenomena she could feel the hot spray carried on the light breeze. Jack was slightly less impressed and already thinking of places to go on their next trip. Maybe even Hell, Michigan, he chuckled to himself. For now he was trying to enjoy what they saw of the 2.2 million acre National Park for the sake of his wife. They had to make the most of their stay for what he was paying for three nights at the Roosevelt Lodge in the park.

***

Henry and Marjorie McCall were on their tenth trip to Yellowstone and were enjoying the scenery just as much as ever. They loved every minute of their trips and, now they were in their seventies, they wanted to savour every single moment they still had together, knowing that every trip could be the last for one of them although both were in reasonably good health so they hoped they may have many years and a few more vacations together. Yellowstone was Henry's favourite place on earth.

***

Klaus Ferber and his girlfriend, Anneke Fischer had saved for the trip to Yellowstone for over two years. They had arrived from Hamburg just a few days previously. They had met at university in the city, both studying Geology, and found they had a mutual love for volcanoes. The walls of their small flat in the centre of Hamburg were covered in posters and prints of the most famous volcanoes in the world. They were already talking about planning a trip to Pompeii in another couple of years. They chose Yellowstone because the active hydrothermal features fascinated them. They had lived together for almost three years and they were talking about getting married as soon as they had their degrees. Plenty of time though.

***

Widower Aaron Buckman and his three young children, Jade, Aaron Junior and Kylee, were taking the trip to de-stress after the slow and painful death of Aaron's wife, Jill, a few weeks previously from bowel cancer. When they got back home they would make plans for a new life for just the four of them. Very probably a move away from Seattle for a fresh start. Aaron worked from home as a day trader so he could move anywhere that he and the kids wanted. All he needed was a good internet connection. The youngsters could have a vote because he knew all three children would probably choose somewhere different but they had to learn to compromise sometime. He thought about Florida, nice weather and he was sure the kids would love to be near Disney World in Orlando. He'd need to do some serious research when he got back home. Try to come up with several possibilities to put to them. Maybe even England, who knew? Seattle had too many memories, some great but recently not so good. He knew it would be hard to get them to agree on somewhere but at least he was open minded about where they would eventually settle. His kid's happiness had to come first... always. For now they were loving every minute of their stay in Yellowstone. The kids loved sleeping in the giant tent Aaron had rented for their stay at one of the many camping grounds. He had always loved nature and was delighted the kids seemed to as well.

***

The massive blast wasn't expected by anyone, least of all the USGS which monitors areas like the Yellowstone caldera. No warnings, no time to evacuate the area safely. An area of roughly 15 by 10 miles erupted and red hot lava and burning ash flew into the air, incinerating everything in its wake instantly. All the hopes and dreams and the memories of everyone in the blast area were gone and forgotten in a flash. Strangely the pyroclastic cloud only travelled East and the ash cloud reached a ceiling of less than 15,000 feet before stopping and falling to earth again. It seemed to the investigators weeks later that the eruption was very controlled because the potential devastation could have potentially killed billions worldwide if the explosion had behaved as expected.

***

The pyroclastic wave destroyed everything in its path, choking the nearby towns of Cody, Powell and Lovell together with Greybull to the East and Worland and Thermopolis to the South of Greybull. Far worse devastation was halted by the famous Bighorn Mountains further east. The towns of Sheridan and Buffalo were luckily untouched by the disaster, though. More than 45,000 died in the affected towns and around a thousand tourists and staff perished inside the park. The largest nearby town of Casper was relatively untouched by the flow as it was funnelled by the mountain range mainly away from its direction and most of the sixty thousand residents survived. But everything there was covered in six inches of the coarse volcanic dust. In all, almost fifty thousand Americans and a few dozen foreign tourists died that day from the eruption and countless more would suffer from respiratory problems for the rest of their lives. This was the biggest disaster in American history and the world's media went into a complete frenzy, trying to scare the people as to what would happen next. But then the media are always trying to terrify everyone for one reason or another - it sells their newspapers and the advertising on their websites. Fear sells... it always has.

London.
July 19th.

Prime Minister Robert Garland walked briskly along to the private Comms room in Downing Street. He'd got an urgent call from the US a few minutes previously requesting an urgent video link up with the US President, Darnell Best, a brash, rude and forceful man even at the best of times. Garland had been dreading it ever since he'd heard the incredibly sad reports of the devastation at Yellowstone Park. He used his key card to enter the Comms room and quietly closed the door behind him and then sat in the plush leather chair in front of an eighty inch screen fixed to the far wall. He steeled himself by taking a deep breath and then used the remote control to open the video link. He saw the President sitting behind a desk in a similar room at the White House, red faced as if he's just chewed out one of his many minions. His normally pristine hair slightly out of place.

"Bob, glad you can make the time for this call, this is a real shit show, isn't it?" said the large blond man on the screen. He was wearing an immaculate dark grey suit, white shirt and a red tie and, for once, looked almost lost for words. Garland had never seen him this agitated during the close to the six and a half years of his Presidency. He'd sailed through the Iranian crisis two years previously in a cool way even Clint Eastwood couldn't replicate. He'd tamed North Korea, some said by diplomacy, though his critics said it was bullying, and had a good relationship with the Russian leader. He was the most popular President since Kennedy but Best knew his stock would fall sharply after this National catastrophe.

"Yes, Darn. My condolences to you and your country from me and from the British people. It must be like 9/11 all over again. Obviously you'll get all the help and support we can possibly give," replied Garland.

"What we need is to find this Mother Earth and put a real good stop to that son of a bitch." Best was close to tears. "This is 9/11, Pearl Harbor, the San Francisco quake and every other tragedy in America all rolled into one, worse even, and we've never known anything like it. No one has. The logistics are already a goddam nightmare, Bob," he said.

"This is really getting out of hand, Darn. Our GCHQ and your guys at the Pentagon are working around the clock together to find who or what is causing all this. The usual suspects, Russia, China and the North Koreans all deny it is them and there is certainly no evidence any of them are involved, even if none of them have been hit by one of these major disasters. Iran are not capable after we virtually neutralised the whole country between us two years ago. No - I don't think it is any country, which means that it is either some individual or radical terrorist group with amazingly advanced technological expertise or, and I am loathe to say this, a real supernatural entity... really Mother Earth," sighed Garland.

"Whoever, or whatever, is causing this, they will pay for it - one way or another, by God," growled an agitated Best.

"I agree, full force, Darn. Millions have been killed worldwide, so far. Who knows where another disaster will strike and how much worse it could be. Yellowstone was totally devastating but we could be in for something even worse," said Garland.

"You're forgetting Paris, Bob" sighed Best.

"I don't think anyone could forget Paris, Darn. I just meant we don't know what lengths this could escalate to. Tens of millions, a billion? More? We just have no idea and usually no have no warnings. One interesting thing though, Darn. This Mother Earth seems to be communicating mainly with one person in particular. A British Youtube vlogger called Steve Hansen. Now, we've checked him out thoroughly and he seems pretty clean, speeding fines mostly, but why him? What we've found is he's forty-four, both parents dead, the father died before he was born. No siblings. Divorced with no children. Just a typical working class man. There must be something about him, though. I don't think this is just random and we're still digging, but we've come up with nothing substantial so far."

"I'd haul the son of a bitch in. Nothing over the top, just an informal chat to find out what he knows and if he has any idea why he has been the main point of contact for this Mother Earth," urged Best.

"Yes, I already have Darn. He apparently knows nothing tangible and had no idea why this terrorist keeps contacting him. I believe him to be honest,

Darn. At the moment he's still under surveillance. We're obviously taking no chances with him. He seems to spend most of his time in his office, which doubles as his studio, and at the local pub, both with his friend Peter Marshall, an ex-BBC employee who is the tech man of the Youtube operation. We've also checked Marshall out and, like Hansen, seems clean, married, no kids, parents retired and live in Devon. His wife has a sister, that's about it, Darn," said Garland.

"Okay, keep me informed of any updates, Bob," Best smiled grimly. "We'll get this son of a bitch. We have to. Meanwhile I'll organise another video conference for the world leaders to discuss Intel, options and what we can do to placate whoever is causing this, even if it's just to string them along for a while until we get them."

"Sounds good, Darn. Good luck with the aftermath of Yellowstone. As I said, you have our full support, as always. Talk to you soon."

Garland left the Comms room and walked to his private office. He poured himself a large thirty-five year old single malt, sat at his desk and sighed heavily. He had a press conference in an hour. His advisors still hadn't formulated anything that will convey the real horror of what was happening or any real plan of action. He closed his eyes and sighed again. He knew his career was on the line at best. Just how far can, or will, this 'Mother Earth' be prepared to go? And more importantly, how much longer before the majority of British voters start to call for his head?

***

Vera Castle sat at her kitchen table reading one of her daily newspapers, five of them in all, which some poor boy had to cycle over four miles to deliver to the old farmhouse she lived in. She felt sorry for him but she had to read as many news sources as she could to keep up with the latest developments around the world. Mostly she used the internet but realised that a lot of the content being suppressed or was just there to sell something - either a product or an agenda. At least in print she could avoid most of that. She used a lot of alternative news sites where you really got the truth. Apparently the US President broke down in tears addressing the media after the Yellowstone eruption. She thought he was a damn hypocrite. His inaction, as well as many of the other world leaders, meant he had blood on his own hands too. Yellowstone had been a real test for her powers. She was pleased she was able to control the blast. Not just the radius, but the direction of it too. She made sure that the ash clouds did not rise too high and block out the sun because that would have caused even more problems for the planet. Her goal was to save the world and not make things worse, like all those ineffective and corrupt governments were doing. Well, it wasn't the governments totally at fault really, was it? - it was mainly the big businesses causing the pollution but the governments were always turning a blind eye. The corporations were spending less on controlling their disgusting polluted waste and their focus was ever increasing profit. The government raked in the extra corporation taxes from that profit and that had satisfied them in the past. Money was the key to it all - ever since the Industrial Revolution hundreds of years ago. Waste from the cotton mills and other factories were released into the rivers. It was just the very start. The start of killing nature and the whole damn planet. She would put a stop to it - whatever it took.

Melbourne, Australia.
July 26th.

Michael Cameron was silently sitting, deep in thought and self-pity, on a cold steel bench outside the court. Sat next to him was Janie Smith, secretary, best friend and occasional lover. He was nervously waiting there, trying to delay the inevitable - finalising his impending bankruptcy case. He owned, for the moment, a new car dealership but business has been bad for a couple of years and then he gambled by buying a better class of stock, mainly electric vehicles, trying to attract people who actually had money to spare and were woke enough to spend it. He was fifty-two and divorced many years previously with four grown up kids ranging from twenty to twenty-six - all living their own happy little lives. He thought his life, as he knew it, was pretty much over... finished. He'd lose the business and his house - all his assets would be used to pay off the debts incurred by the failed car business. He'd have nothing left, losing all he had worked bloody hard for over the years.

He supposed he could move in with Janie - he knew she would offer, but thought that would be a bad idea. They had known each other for about twenty-five years since he had opened the showroom back in the late nineties. God, she was certainly a looker back in the day, still not bad, even now. It was just him as a salesman, Janie running the office side of things and Darren and Joe, his mechanics, and the business had grown steadily from there, now employing twelve people. He had been successful, but everyone was financially worse off now and the new car market was virtually on its knees. People were going for good second-hand cars or making their current vehicles last a bit longer. No one could afford to buy a new car in the current financial climate. He really should have bought better, affordable second-hand stock and gone in that direction instead, rather than using his borrowed capital buying models upwards of $200k. He had realised that stocking electric cars was a mistake. He thought they were just a fad now. How could they be so green if they are still charged with electricity made from fossil fuels? Michael was many things but he truly believed he was not an idiot and easily duped like the rest of the public into falling for the 'climate con' as he called it, but he did think all his potential customers were. He doubted if he would be sitting there now next to Janie, outside a bloody court, if he'd just stuck to what worked in the past - good cars at good prices. He really feared for the future now that he'd blown it. He'd have to get a job in another showroom because selling cars was all he knew. But most places were in the same boat as him - a total downturn in the market was killing the motor trade. Shit! He'd thought about ending it all, but that would be hard on his kids. Ha! Kids? They were grown adults now. He doubted if they even cared about him anymore after his string of affairs had totally destroyed their mother's life. They were civil to him, usually just phone calls on his birthday or at Christmas, but he knew they didn't love him anymore and hadn't since they had been teenagers during the break up of his marriage. Just as well the ex-wife had got the house after the divorce. It would just be another asset he'd be losing. And she would have been homeless as well as him. She didn't deserve that, she had done nothing wrong. He realised thing had started to go very wrong for him long before the business had started to fail. He had never thought of himself as a loser before.

Michael felt a slight rumble beneath his feet but didn't feel too concerned. He was in the city in 2021 when a relatively minor earthquake hit - it caused a little bit of damage to buildings but no loss of life. He was actually hoping the court building behind him would collapse and delay the proceedings for a few weeks or months but he would never be that lucky. He looked at Janie and she returned a tight smile. She was just as nervous because she realised she'd be out of work too.

"Mike, I've been thinking. Why don't you move-"

Then an ear splitting 'CRACK' filled their heads. More loud rumbles, a lot more powerful this time. The tall office blocks in the distance on the other side of the wide street started to sway horribly from side to side. Windows in front of them and behind them shattered, the tinkling of glass sounded like a million wind chimes. They could hear the screams from the people in the buildings over all the devastatingly terrifying noise. The courthouse behind them crumbled, crushing hundreds of mostly innocent people inside. The offices opposite them wobbled again and then collapsed forwards onto the slowly moving cars below, killing even more blameless commuters. The overhead street lights fell down and crushed people in their cars who had all stopped in the road unsure of what to do and were now starting to panic. Then the entire road disappeared - just fell like a giant out of control concrete and tarmac elevator. There was a massively wide chasm where the main street used to be. Devastation was all around them, apart from the small green space in front of the rubble of the courthouse, where they both sat clinging grimly to the cold steel bench. The small area amazingly remained untouched by the earthquake. The rumbling and the crashing of buildings gradually tailed off only to be replaced by dozens of screams and the groans of those who had somehow survived the havoc and ruin of Melbourne. Countless sirens sounded in the distance. Dozens of fire alarms filled the air. It felt very eerie to those who were left in shock. The city they had loved was totally decimated.

Michael and Janie just stared at each other in shock - the shock not only due to the incident but that they had both amazingly survived intact. Thick dust swirled all around them, diffusing the usually bright natural sunlight above. Michael tried to rise from his seated position but then he felt dizzy and immediately sat down again heavily. His chest felt very tight and a severe pain radiated down his left arm. Sweat started to drip from him, his scalp was saturated with it. He could hardly breathe. He could feel his life ebbing away as Janie sat frozen, gripping the metal bench in panic, unable to do anything to help him.

Michael Cameron was never a very lucky man.

Over nine-thousand Australians died that day in Melbourne, a relatively minor number compared to other earthquakes all around the world, but considering that none of the continent lay over any tectonic plates, making earthquakes very rare and minor, it was just another massive mystery. All of Australia was in shock and mourning for their fellow countrymen and women.

London.
July 27th.

"So what I'll do is just introduce the two of you, we'll have a little informal chat and then do a Q&A using the live comments, is that okay, guys?"

They both nodded their agreement, looking very comfortable in the leather office chairs Steve had picked up from a local charity shop earlier that morning. It was the first time he'd done a live podcast with any guests, let alone two at the same time. Pete had rigged up a couple of extra microphones and had just done level checks to test if their voices were being picked up well enough. After a thumbs up from Pete, Steve leaned in towards his own mike and started.

"Good day, good people. We have something very unique for you all this fine early afternoon. We have a couple of special guests, so that is why I've delayed the broadcast until today. I hope you all saw the announcement earlier in the day informing you of this live feed, but obviously you can catch up on the full show later on Youtube, and now Rumble, if you like. So, first off, I'll introduce my guests before we get into it. Furthest away from me, is a man most of my audience is familiar with, well known conspiracy debunker, Dan French, AKA Danny Fresh Meat. I'm sure he has his own thoughts about what seems to be happening all over the world, with 'Mother Earth' claiming to be responsible for all these disasters, the latest in Australia yesterday. I'm looking forward to hearing his slant on things. Good to see you, Dan."

"Good to be here, Steve," smiled Dan. He didn't really want to be there in truth but knew it would probably boost his own subscribers.

"Last, but certainly not least, a man who I literally owe my life to, horror author Mark Mason, who was with me on the TV panel show, The Agenda. I'm sure you've all seen the footage of the events on the news or social media by now. So if you are not a fan of his books yet then buy one and give him a go. I've got them all and will be cheeky later and get Mark to sign them all for me," grinned Steve.

"Thanks, Steve, very relieved that we both could be here today, our fellow panellists weren't so lucky. I'd have done the same for anyone to be honest, as I'm sure you would too," smiled Mark, trying to play down the hero tag he'd been

saddled with over the last few weeks by the media. It had done wonders for sales and he had made a couple of chat show appearances though, so he hadn't been complaining. Although it did keep him away from his wife, Natalie... Especially as she was pregnant with their first child. One appearance was in the same studio as The Agenda and anyone who watched closely would have seen him repeatedly look nervously towards the patched up ceiling while being questioned by the very camp interviewer, Gary Green, whose real name was a rather dull Fred Pickles, his thick Yorkshire accent almost masked by his effeminate nasal drone. Green reminded him of White, the equally annoying Mancunian sidekick of his best friend D.I. Gerry Daly. Gerry had featured in his first three books over the last couple of years, and probably would again. He usually investigated the strange events around Kingsford where they both lived. Hopefully no more demons now that Anrok was thankfully dead by his own hand.

"Okay, let's get right into it and don't forget to keep the comments coming, and my guests will do their best to answer your questions for you. So, let's recap. These disasters all over the world are apparently being caused by someone or something going by the slightly ominous name of 'Mother Earth' and to be honest I'm not too sure if this is a person, a group or indeed, a supernatural entity. In my mind though, whoever or whatever they are, they do exist and if you've seen the show where Pete and I experienced a localised earth tremor and me being hit in the face by the mike it convince me, at least. It was very localised, I may add, because it only seemed to happen in our studio and we were the only two affected. Sadly, so many people have died all over the world... it's not just Britain anymore. The death tolls have ranged from a couple of dozen like those poor boys gassed at a school in Kent to around five million souls in Paris. So devastating, and very much a worry for everyone, I'm sure. Your thoughts, Dan?"

"Well, as you well know from my own show, I'm a natural skeptic, and try to see reason and logic where there may not apparently be any. Yes, these disasters are awful, but every single one can be explained as a natural occurrence in my opinion. Earthquakes, tsunamis, gas pockets, even the sudden freeze in Paris have all happened before in various parts of the world throughout history. I think the person calling themselves 'Mother Earth' is just a sick, attention seeking freak who is taking credit for all these natural events. I'll admit, the fact that they are all happing in such a short space of time is most unusual but not impossible in my

considered judgment. There may have been a similar sequence far back in our history that was never recorded... especially before man, or should I say people to be totally politically correct, existed. "

"Interesting take, Dan. But Mother Earth has actually predicted a few of these events a few days in advance in advance. Western Europe for the Paris freeze and London panel show, for example. How do you explain that?" asked Steve.

"It's the law of averages, Steve," replied Dan quite smugly. *"We've all seen or read about these so-called psychics. They are deliberately vague about all their predictions and take all the credit they can get after something accidentally fits their 'prediction.'"* Dan did his trademark 'air quotes' with his fingers. *"We have thousands of people attributing many things to the words of Nostradamus, but his works are basically vague poems that could mean anything if you really put your mind to it. I mean, the 'fire from the sky' one. 9/11? Come on, that's a bit of a stretch even for those Nostradumbers as I call them. Any one of us could make these bold statements and sooner or later we'd all get a 'hit'. It's just luck, really. I could predict that Tottenham Hotspur will win a trophy one day, although to be honest it could take a while for me to be proven right,"* chuckled Dan.

"Don't get Pete's hopes up, Dan," laughed Steve. *"He's been a long suffering fan that particular club since he was a kid."* Steve winked at Pete from behind his microphone.

"But you get the point, don't you, Steve?" pressed Dan. *"Every vague prediction could possibly come true if you give it enough time and wait for the right event to crop up and get a match and even then the link could be very tenuous and even more subjective."*

"Yes, I have to concede that is a logical explanation and you've put your case very well, Dan. I hope some of the comments will actually agree with you so that we get a balanced opinion from our viewers, and I'm sure there will be a few of your subscribers tuning in to give you a bit of support." Steve smiled. *"We're all about fairness on this channel. It's really what this show is all about, isn't it? An exchange of ideas from the subscribers and, if possible, some explanations. But we do have a huge mystery going on and we need as many minds and as many intelligent conversations as we can get to try and explain what is happening,"* said Steve. *"Now, Mark Mason, what are your thoughts on this?"*

"Well, Steve, being a writer, I have to mainly rely on my imagination and try and think outside the box when it comes to explaining things, either a strange

plot or the motivation and actions of a particular character, good or bad. I do appreciate where Dan is coming from, though I have to disagree with him. I, as you are painfully aware, was almost a victim of that incident in the BBC studio. One of the events predicted by this 'Mother Earth' - the location and method were both correct. No pun intended, but thinking about it really gives me chills," said Mark, smiling at what really was a pun. *"I think we really need to take all this very seriously and I firmly believe that whatever is happening is really caused, or at least influenced, by this person or thing, Mother Earth. I know there are things out there that are really difficult to explain rationally, but we should accept and respect what they are. As you know, as you've read the books, that I have experienced a lot of strange events, including a witch and a demon. A group of friends have even tackled an immortal serial killer while I was in America. That tale was told in my second book, A Rip in Time, do forgive the plug, Steve."* Mark grinned.

"Not a problem Mark. It is a great story. Now both sides have put across well it's time we looked at a few comments, chaps," said Steve.

Six Kids And Have To Stop: It's the end of the fucking world, lads!

"Well, we all hope it's not as drastic as that, Six Kids. I do get that many people are very worried about what we may be left with after all of this is finished... if indeed it does ever finish. But let's try to stay positive, especially for the sake of your little ones. But on the other hand the planet has always survived and healed itself. This world has come a very long way since the asteroid that hit the earth 65 million years ago. It did take hundreds of thousands of years, if not millions, but we are all here, aren't we? Life survived in whatever form it did and then it evolved. Even our ancient ancestors have survived a massive ice age lasting a few thousand years and other things in history, like plagues, floods and so on, so let's not get too down-hearted at the moment, humans are quite resilient when you think about it... Dan?"

"Totally agree there, Steve. Natural disasters with a big capital N!"

"Mark?" said Steve, turning to his other guest.

"Yes, Steve. The planet has always survived... but will mankind? That is the biggest question."

RickAstleyFan: I think it's all down to Climate Change. What do you think, guys?

"LOL - Rick Astley! Just had a flashback!" laughed Steve. *"Thanks for your comment but isn't everything caused by Climate Change now? Even my piles!"*

WeAreAllInTheMatrix: I think it's a load of crap. Just a big coincidence.

"Well, we know that Dan will agree with you but what would be your response to that, Mark?" asked Steve.

"My best friend, Gerry, always says; 'There is no such thing as coincidence', Steve, and I tend to think he's right. Whether it's Karma or Predestination or some higher power, like an all-powerful God, I think that things are meant to happen for whatever reason," smiled Mark. *"And those who read my last book will remember the character of Downey, a true hero and a great friend, who travelled through time to help Destiny along its path a little."* Mark looked sad as he remembered his friend who took him back to the fifth Century to battle the Demon, Anrok and gave his own life to save the author, whose real life experiences were marketed as fiction but were very true.

"Yes, I've read that one and, as you say, Downey really was a hero, Mark, a top bloke," replied Steve. *"Dan, have you read any of Mark's books?"*

"Not really my cup of tea, Steve," grinned Dan. *"I'm not into fantasy. Sorry Mark."*

"No problem. If everyone liked the same type of books, films, food or even sports teams the world would be a very boring place," smiled Mark.

"Totally agree with that, Mark," said Dan. *"And obviously I agree with that comment from the Matrix geezer too.*

MAGA Michigan Man (USMC): Someone should find that Mother Earth person and blow them away. Send in a team of SEALS and just eliminate that fucker like they did with that terrorist A-rab!

"Would it really be that simple? Mark?" asked Steve.

"I don't think it would be. Mother Earth, if real, seems to have immense power and even if they did find them then actually confronting and stopping them may cause even more problems. No, I think we should strive to comply with the demands and actually do something to save the planet, it's probably the best and safest way for all of us in the long run," said Mark.

"Never give in to terrorists," replied Dan. *"I know that may sound like I believe in all this, I don't, but I mean in general. It's always a bad idea in principle to give in to them."*

"I thought for a moment you were changing your mind there, Dan," grinned Steve.

"No. Definitely not, Steve," laughed Dan. "I still firmly believe that it's all a set of freakish natural occurrences, and this person claiming to be responsible is an absolute, attention seeking hoaxer, it's a mental illness, guys. Sad, but true, in my opinion. They certainly belong in a mental institution, permanently in a padded room. Now that's a fact I firmly believe."

"Okay. That's about all we have time for, gentlemen. My thanks to Dan for coming in to give us his very logical thoughts as to the cause of these disasters and to Mark for his more esoterical view of these events. I've really enjoyed the debate and will probably do more of these live shows on various topics in the future. Maybe get a few third rate celebrities on so I can make fun of them. I know you good people love that. This has been really interesting to get opposing thoughts on this crisis we are facing. Thanks very much, guys," Steve smiled at the pair of guests. *"Now Dan has to leave us to get ready for his own podcast later this evening and do have a listen if you haven't in the past. Mark will hang around for a bit so he can sign my copies of his books and have a wee drinkie."*

"My pleasure, Steve, and I'll be sure to give your channel a mention later," said Dan.

"Cheers, Steve, looking forward to that drink, I'll have a listen to your show myself at some point, Dan," smiled Mark.

Pete cut the feed and signalled to Steve that they were off air. "Great show everyone. Thanks for coming in," said Steve. "I think it all went pretty well... and no earthquakes or flying microphones this time, we survived," he grinned, very relieved.

***

Mother Earth had watched the live debate, her fury was starting to get the better of her. She knew she had to calm the hell down. She didn't want to cause a disaster that wasn't planned or give herself a stroke. She had to maintain control of what she was doing and make people listen. Steve Hansen may have started to say the right things at the moment, but he would ultimately pay the price. The sins of the father will be visited upon the son who never even knew him. She had already brought her revenge on his father and she desperately wanted to make Steve Hansen suffer too. But first she had to make an example of that obnoxious little twerp Dan French. What an offensive turd of a man!

***

Dan French wished he'd taken the car to do the podcast with Steve Hansen. All those smelly poor people crammed onto the tube trains and buses like dirty, ignorant little sardines. He hated public transport but parking in London was a nightmare. He'd walked to the filthy underground station near to where Steve's woefully small studio was and then he'd have a short journey by bus to Camden, where he had lived for seven miserable years. It was probably time to get out of there, he thought, move to somewhere a bit up market now that he was pretty successful and had the money to do so. He inwardly complained that the trip on the bus wouldn't be short enough but it was a lot better than walking through the feral streets of London, at risk of mugging or stabbing or even shooting these days. The streets of London were not safe anymore, the Mayor and Metropolitan Police seemed either disinterested or powerless. Even a five minute trip was pretty unbearable on a bus or the tube. The red double-decker was stinking to high heaven, as usual, all those disgustingly dirty, smelly people sat all around him. The seats were exceedingly grimy and stained with God knows what and he was sat next to a tall skinny West Indian who reeked of premium weed. He decided he actually hated most people he came into contact with, especially in the capital, but on the other hand his anti-conspiracy podcast attracted a lot of these mugs, and they were making him very rich. Over a million subscribers now, more than double that Steve Hansen had accumulated, even though only a small percentage of them actually agreed with his views. Most were real conspiracy nuts who did their best to troll him in the comments. Freaks! Every single one of them. Whatever happened to the collective IQ of the population? It was dropping faster than the ex-wife's knickers. Dirty old slapper! He wondered briefly where she was now - probably shacked up with a drug addict or worse.

He was thankful his stop would be next. He was starting to get a little high just sitting next to Snap Dogg or whatever his fricking name was. He pressed the dirty red button on the pole next to him to alert the bearded Eastern European driver that he wanted to get off this Hell Bus and walk the short distance to his flat. He got off the disgusting grimy red double decker and deeply breathed in the slightly, but not by much, fresher air. Christ, London really was a shithole these days. He had to move out before his lungs gave out or he got stabbed or shot. Dan walked along an uneven pavement alongside the dusty, rubbish strewn street, jostling with the everyday scum he detested, fighting his way along to the small courtyard which led to the tall block of private flats.

He finally reached the deserted, slightly cleaner, courtyard area and he decided the first thing he'd do when he was safely inside the flat was to have a long, hot shower. A bloody long one. Fuck those deluded Climate Change protesters who wanted to limit us all to two or three minutes under the fine, cleansing spray. He doubted all those smelly brainwashed university gits even took one minute to shower. Bloody hypocrites. They all complained about pollution yet too thick to realise that they spouted off their climate hate on plastic phones with a lithium battery which cost lives to mine for. Or they super glue their faces to the motorway - did they even realise how super glue was made? Morons! All of them a waste of oxygen in his opinion. No common sense or idea of how things were produced or worked. Were we all supposed to revert back to the Dark ages? Idiots!

As he walked towards the flats the sky was starting to get slightly cloudy. He was happy he'd get safely inside before the predictable summer rain came. Only twenty yards from the door to the foyer to go, then a lift up to the fifth floor and then shut the shitty world out for a few hours until he started his broadcast for the benefit of the conspiracy nutters, and his bank balance, of course. The small patch of sky between him and the entrance a few yards away now looked blacker by the second. It really would be pissing down in a few minutes but was sure he'd make it in time, he thought happily.

He stood transfixed for a few seconds as a searing bolt of lightning hit him squarely on the top of his head. There was a brief moment of excruciating pain. The back of Dan's skull then virtually exploded in a split second. His eyes melted and his ears were quickly burnt away, becoming nothing but charred gristle. His brain fried and expanded until large wide cracks appeared all over what was left of his skinless skull. The rest of his body was covered in deep, excruciating burns. His cardiovascular system shut down almost instantly. Most people do survive a lightning strike, usually suffering no more than burns, but Mother Earth had made sure Dan French would not be included in that statistic. He slumped to the stained ground, onto the filthy grime he despised so much.

No one found his remains for several minutes - not that it made any difference to his chances of survival anyway. Meanwhile, Steve, Pete and Mark Mason were enjoying a nice fifteen year old single malt. They were oblivious - for now - of the fate of the skeptical guest.

Vera Castle smiled at the TV screen later that evening. A freak weather accident had killed a well-known and popular podcaster. Maybe others will now realise that no one made fun of Mother Earth! She tried to think about the inevitable fate of Steve Hansen, how would she do it? She didn't know yet but it had to be something very creative... just as his father had perished. She knew one thing for sure - Steve Hansen would suffer greatly. And it wouldn't be over as quickly as it was for that disgusting Dan French. French fried! She was almost in hysterics at her own joke. He had his chips! The tears of laughter rolled down her cheeks and on to her faded green cardigan. She hadn't laughed this much in years. It had put a smile on her face that had lasted for the rest of the evening.

Tarbela Dam.
Khyber province, Pakistan.
July 30th.

The old giant dam stood majestically above the dry valley below. Over one hundred and six million cubic metres of water held back by the wide concrete structure which was filled by earth and rock between its thick walls. The hydro electric machinery produced nearly fourteen thousand GWh - just one Gigawatt could power one hundred million LED bulbs for a year and the seventeen turbines installed could easily power the whole region of the Indus valley as well as providing millions of gallons of water for the irrigation of the farmland below. The only downside was the two hundred million tons of sediment per year building up in the bottom of the reservoir as the source of the water was the glacial melt from the Himalayas which collected the silt in its run-off. The silt was constantly dredged from the bottom, a 24/7 operation, otherwise the capacity of the dam would be severely reduced in just a few months.

Sarfraz Malik was the lone caretaker on duty at the dam. Normally his job was to sweep up the fine dust that fell from the walls in the maintenance tunnels that ran through the dam and also any cleaning that needed to be done. He was now fifty-six and had worked at the dam since he was a small boy during its construction. The money wasn't much but at least he had a job to feed his large family and he regarded the dam as 'his' - a part of him, a great part of his whole life. He maybe loved the dam more than his six sons and two daughters. Well, more than his daughters for sure.

He had noticed there was more of the white dust in the tunnels than was usual. A little surprising as the dam originally had a working life of around fifty years but a series of much smaller dams up river was supposed to take a lot of strain away and extend the life of the Tarbela to more than eighty-five years. Sarfraz knew he would be long gone when the dam was eventually decommissioned. He would hate to see that day come during his own lifetime.

Sarfraz was suddenly rocked violently and thrown to the dusty floor. He looked up at the dull, faded white walls of the tunnel. Dozens of cracks then appeared, widening by the second. "Naheen, Naheen, Naheen," he cried out, not believing what he was seeing. He tried to get up but another tremor threw him onto his back again as a block of concrete weighing several tons fell from the roof of the tunnel and mercilessly crushed him out of existence.

The dam took less than thirty seconds to completely disintegrate. Millions of gallons of water cascaded into the valley. Nearby farming villages were swept away without any warning, the towns further away had very little time to evacuate and even the city of Karachi, further away, failed to survive the flood. Millions of people were swept into the Arabian Sea. It was impossible to calculate the death toll but conservative estimates were in the region of fifty million lost. As the news circulated the world the full horror and devastation was barely comprehensible. A whole region was under water. Very few countries were able to give aid as they were having to cope with their own disasters, both major and minor. Then the inevitable related diseases came. Typhoid and cholera killed millions more over the next few months. Nothing could be done to save the unfortunate victims. The whole planet was now in total chaos.

***

London.
July 31st.

Steve Hansen was taking a rare morning off to relax and recharge his batteries after hearing of the death of fellow Youtuber Dan French and the dam violently bursting apart in Pakistan. Was Dan's demise a freak accident? Steve knew for sure that it seemed those who doubted the power Mother Earth had bad things happen to them. Did she create the lightning that killed him before he got to the safety of his flat? According to the Met. Office it was the only lightning strike in London that day. What are the odds that it would hit the one person who was very critical of Mother Earth on Steve's channel? What convinced Steve was that Dan outright scoffed and insulted Mother Earth... even called 'her' an attention seeking hoaxer and a mentally ill freak! Steve needed to stress on the next show of the dangers of that. Just in case it was true. He didn't want to be next - the microphone incident was more than enough for him. He was lying on the cool black leather couch in the office/studio with his headphones on, trying to forget about the last few days. He was in an Eighties Hair Rock mood. Whitesnake gave way to Warrant, Accept, W.A.S.P. and Don Dokken. His eyes were lightly closed as the MP3 player on his phone moved on to Twisted Sister. *We're not Gonna Take It* seemed very apt under the circumstances, but what could they do to stop Mother Earth? Steve felt a hand on his shoulder and sat up, startled, his heart racing. Pete was standing over him with a worried look on his face.

"Shit, Pete!" cried Steve. "Don't fucking do that, you knob! You almost scared the life out of me!"

"Sorry, mate," said Pete. I know I was going to leave you alone today but something came up."

"Couldn't you bloody call me?" Steve's heart was finally beginning to slow down after the initial shock. It definitely was not the relaxing day he'd planned on when he'd left his flat that morning.

"Didn't think, mate. Sorry. Anyway, the wife's sister, Jane, visited last night and she wants to help."

"How the hell can your sister in law possibly be of assistance? You always said she was a bit of a weirdo, didn't you?"

"Well, she is a bit," Pete grinned. "But I think it may be worth a shot, mate. We were talking last night about how Mother Earth can stay anonymous all the time and she thinks she can maybe track her or them down," he smiled. His initial embarrassment now turning to guarded enthusiasm.

"I didn't know there was any bloodhound in your wife's ancestry. Is she related to Scooby Doo too?" scoffed Steve.

"No, just listen for a minute, Steve. She says she's psychic or clairvoyant or something. I'm not really up on these things. Jackie backed her up though. She told me about a load of weird stuff from when they were kids. She was well known for finding missing stuff like lost keys or cats trapped in sheds."

"Well, if your wife recommends her as a bounty hunter then that settles it, doesn't it!" laughed Steve. "Are you pulling my plonker or are you bloody serious, Pete?"

"Have you got any better ideas?" asked Pete. "Besides, she's a nice girl and maybe you two could hit it off. She's dying to meet you. Jackie has actually been singing your praises for once."

"Oh great, now you are trying to fix me up with a bloody hippy weirdo, can today get any worse, Pete?"

"Just think of her as interesting and not weird, Steve. I don't think she's that much of a hippy either, just a bit 'earthy' if you know what I mean? Honestly, I think you would like her. And consider this - what if she really can trace where Mother Earth is? How cool would that be?" beamed Pete?

"Remind me why we are still friends?" groaned Steve.

"Okay. So you'll drop round later this evening? Have a talk with her? I'll order an Indian."

"I hope you mean food and not some fucking Swami or Fakir? I never know with you these days. Okay, I'll be there. About eight?"

"Perfect. Sorted."

"Yes, sorted. Now piss off and let me relax a bit, Pete," he growled.

Pete grinned and quietly left the office while Steve settled back on the couch and replaced his headphones and clicked on his MP3 player for the next random track. Iron Maiden were now blasting out The Clairvoyant. Steve inwardly groaned yet again. At least he'd get a decent meal out of it, he thought. He started to wonder what Jackie's sister was like.

***

Later that evening Steve nervously walked up the garden path and rang the doorbell. It was one minute past eight. He didn't want to seem too keen to those inside, especially Jackie's sister. He was far from it but he did want to give the girl a chance though. Plenty of "what ifs" had clumsily blundered their way around the inside of his head all that afternoon. He was dressed in a t-shirt and jeans, mainly to avoid the other three thinking this was some sort of a proper date. It was just a casual takeaway night with friends in his mind, but he was sure that Pete and Jackie had other ideas and were hoping he and this Jane girl really hit it off. He sort of thought the same but had no real expectations. It may turn out he would dislike her within about five minutes like that last girl Pete had tried to fix him up with. Janice, one of Jackie's friends from work, was a complete nutter and it took a while to convince her that he would never be interested in her. She even followed him through the streets once. His first stalker. Hopefully his last. Now he was even more nervous, dreading a repeat of that little fiasco.

Pete opened the door and invited his best friend in. Jackie gave him a hug as she always did and he sat down at one end of a light brown fabric three seater. Perched at the other end was a pretty red haired woman with lovely green eyes. She looked totally different from her sister, who was tall and slim with long blond hair. Jane was by no means chubby - far from it - but looked a pretty normal size to him. He didn't really like skinny girls. Jackie exited to the kitchen where she grabbed a cold Stella for Steve, which he gratefully accepted. She then sat in one of a pair of matching leather armchairs with Pete sprawled in the other.

"This is my baby sister, Jane. But you've probably guessed that by now, Steve," said Jackie, smiling.

"I had an inkling," grinned Steve. "I'm pleased to meet you, Jane." He held out his hand and Jane took it lightly in her own. Her skin was quite cold to the touch. Nerves? She smiled at him and her eyes shone back.

"Jackie's told me a lot about you, Steve," she said, almost blushing.

"Only the good stuff, I hope," grinned Steve. Lucky Pete hasn't told you all the bad things or you wouldn't be here."

"Are there bad things, Steve?" asked the redhead, looking interested.

"Just the usual. Bad jobs, bad marriage, bad feet, bad jokes," he smiled.

"Nothing the rest of us haven't been through then. No marriage, just a few dickhead boyfriends. It's weird, I can sense what a lot of people are really like but I never could with them."

"Pete mentioned you had a sort of gift. A few months ago I would have been quite skeptical about stuff like that but with this Mother Earth thing going on I've become a lot more open minded. At least I don't dismiss things out of hand now, which has to be good. I'm not too old to adapt and evolve, I suppose."

"You're not too old at all," Jane smiled.

Steve decided he liked her.

"So," Steve continued, trying not to let the flirting get in the ways of business, "Pete says you may be able to help us get a lead on this Mother Earth? Maybe track their location down. Please tell me more," he smiled warmly, now totally at ease.

"Pete told me that sometimes when you are doing your podcast she or they sometimes interact with you. I know you get emails but they are not really live. Pete says they bounce all over the place before they get to you, but the messages during a live stream are pretty instant, he tells me. I'd love to try to trace one of those if I you'll let me."

"It would just mean that she sits next to me when we broadcast and tries to pick up anything coming through the tech. So she wouldn't actually be in front of the camera," said Pete.

"So no Beauty and the Beast episode then," joked Steve. "Okay, so I just get onto the subject of the disasters and then try and goad this Mother Earth to chip in with some sort of comment or reaction so Jane can try and track her?"

"That's pretty much it, mate. So hopefully Jane can pick up their location, it may be only a rough area but it would at least be a start and then we can pass on that information to the government," confirmed Pete. "Then they can take their shit off my bloody PC."

"Sounds good. One thing though. I was thinking earlier that those people who cross Mother Earth tend to meet with an accident or even a sticky end like

Dan French did. What is actually stopping her from finding out what we are plotting and eradicate us all before we find her?" asked Steve.

"Good point," said Pete. "But I'm not sure there is anything we can do to prevent it, really. We just have to trust to luck and hope she doesn't find out. Jane is willing to take the risk to try and stop all this shit and I think we should too. Millions are dying and there could be countless millions more - even potentially the rest of the human race, so I think we owe it to everyone to at least try, Steve."

"All right, but if your head explodes don't come running to me," laughed Steve. Jane laughed too. That's a good sign, he thought, laughing at his bad jokes. He hoped it wasn't just her politeness. He definitely liked her.

The rest of the evening was nice and relaxing. The Indian takeaway was very good. Steve was impressed that Jane seemed to like spicy food. The small talk was interesting after Steve stopped annoying everyone with his Silly Fakir quips. Lots of stories from the childhood of the two sisters including the time that sister Jackie had fallen in a pond when she was supposed to be grounded and Jane was tasked with trying to distract their parents while Jackie climbed a tree on the other side of the house to get in through her bedroom window. Their mother knew exactly what was going on because a neighbour was giving her a running commentary of Jackie's efforts on her newly bought Nokia mobile phone. Her mother was trying not to laugh at Jane's relentless questions about which animal would win a race between each other. The goldfish versus a rabbit was the last straw and prompted the mother to ask Jane to run upstairs to collect her sister's wet clothes. Jane finally worked out the game was up and scuttled up the stairs to tell Jackie their mum knew she'd been found out and was probably in a lot of trouble for sneaking out while she was grounded. Neither could actually agree on what Jackie had done to get herself in trouble in the first place. Jackie thought it was playing truant, while Jane thought Jackie had been too cheeky to their parents which was probably more believable to Steve.

Pete told Jane a few embarrassing stories about Steve and their nights out in the past. Steve actually didn't mind her knowing that he could be a bit of an idiot when he was stupidly drunk. Most stories ended with him and Pete buying kebabs and passing out on a park bench. Steve assured her that it was all in their younger days and he was more mature now. Jane giggled, helped by the second bottle of white wine she and her sister were sharing. Steve was delighted it had been a good night. Good enough that he asked Jane if she would go out for a meal sometime in the near future. Jane accepted without any hesitation, which Steve found very encouraging. He was usually a bit awkward when meeting new people, especially women, but felt totally at ease with Jane. The night ended with hugs all around and Steve left at around midnight and walked the two miles to his flat, not even bothering to call for a taxi. He smiled a lot on the way home as he thought about Jane.

Pete and the two girls sat up for another hour, mostly talking about Steve and how well he got on with Jane. Pete was impressed that a professional procrastinator like his friend had actually asked Jane out the first time he had met her. Jane had told the others that she had instantly liked Steve and had been picking up good vibes from him all evening. She thought he was a nice guy but tried very hard not to show that side of him too often. Pete agreed with that without hesitation. He told her his best friend usually tried to distance himself from most people and thought that it was great that they had both got on so well and Steve seemed to open up readily to Jane. It had been a great evening for all of them.

Scottish Highlands.
August 2nd.

The majestic lone deer crossed the windswept deserted road. There was virtually no danger as a car had not been along that stretch for nearly two hours, the Highland road was so remote - at least fifty miles from any of the remote towns in the region. The large animal calmly reached the other side of the highway and brushed against some bone dry ferns and heather, feeling a slight tickle and scraping on its left flank. The severe drought earlier in the year had even reached the normally moist and fertile Highlands and a lot of the wild animals in the area had died from dehydration. The water levels in the lochs were down several feet from the usual seasonal mark. The dry, browned slope in front of the deer was dotted with dozens of sheep, all lazily roaming around trying to find even a tiny patch of greenery to eat. Luckily for the local farmers these sheep were used for wool production because there wasn't much meat on them anymore and that meat would be stringy and tasteless anyway. The deer pushed his snout high into the air, sniffing at the slightly warm breeze. A strong scent was quickly travelling towards him. A smell he'd experienced a long time ago when he'd been nothing but a small fawn. It wasn't a good smell. His heart started to race as he remembered what it was. He didn't know the name of it but he knew that if he didn't run he would die like a lot of the herd in the past. A wave of extreme heat enveloped him now and he quickly turned and ran. Back across the road he went. Not stopping until he was exhausted and safe, breathless from the warm, fetid air. He could see a large dark cloud in the distance with bright colours emanating from the bottom. Reds and yellows. His instinct told him that those colours were bad and to stay away from them.

The fires in the Highlands didn't take many lives but, even in such a remote area, caused a lot of damage to farmland and the scattered properties. At first arson was blamed but that was quickly dismissed due to the drought conditions and the only criminal act was probably someone throwing a lit cigarette from a car window as they drove to Inverness or Fort William, the culprit would have been impossible to trace. The real truth was that it was another example of the power of Mother Earth.

It took a dozen fire engines and their crews almost a week to get the heathland fires under control. More devastation, more resources used and another show of strength, although unknown by anyone else but Vera Castle.

***

London.
August 3rd.

The Boeing 737 followed the normal flight path from Wayne County, Detroit to Gatwick Airport in England. It was just a routine flight. The captain, forty-three year old Marcus Watson, was looking forward to landing and taking a few days off with his wife and two teenage children before the kids went back to school after the summer break. His co-pilot, James Scott, was only twenty-five and newly qualified and was only on his third ever flight. They were both going through the in-flight landing checks as they were less than ten minutes from Gatwick and were preparing for stacking and waiting their turn to land. They were flying directly over London when all hell broke loose. Every alarm went off at the same time. Every system was failing. Both engines had stopped with no warning - the turbines seized solid. The captain used all his experience to try and restart them while Scott was in emergency communication with Gatwick Air Traffic Control tower. Gatwick tower were trying to create a slot for them to try and coast in and land. Watson prayed the landing gear would work. Despite the ATC's assurance that it could be done, Scott had started to panic. Captain Watson tried to calm him down while still trying to start the twin jets again. Behind the locked cockpit door he could hear the passengers start to scream in panic. They had noticed the stopped engines and the rapid decrease in altitude. Captain Watson had to focus. He knew they could still coast in if he could maintain a decent altitude for the last few miles and Gatwick could clear a runway pretty quickly - he just had to keep things together for a few more minutes, but his co-pilot freaking out wasn't helping him at all. Then, to his horror, all forward momentum of the plane suddenly stopped. For a couple of seconds it felt like the aircraft was just hovering in mid-air, like it was being held by a giant invisible hand. Then it dropped like a stone towards the city of London below.

Unaware of what was happening above, the England football team were playing a World Cup qualifying match at Wembley Stadium against lowly San Marino and were already five goals to the good early into the second half.

Almost ninety thousand cheering fans were packed into the stadium and they all looked up as one when the eighty ton Boeing crashed through the arch over the roof and then onto the seating and pitch. The loss to English football eclipsed every other disaster in the football world. More than eighty thousand dead including every one of the players on the pitch and benches. All either crushed by debris or immolated by burning jet fuel. The explosion would have been a lot worse if the plane hadn't been almost out of the liquid. British football would never recover after losing over three billion pounds worth of talent as well as the national stadium. Once again, the nation mourned a massive loss.

London.
August 4th.

After one of the worst days in British history, the media were targeting Prime Minister Robert Garland, as they do. Blaming him for the terrible catastrophes befalling the country as if a change of leadership of the unpopular Conservative government would solve problems like an airliner dropping out of the sky onto a football stadium. The papers had riled up the other MPs so much that a vote of no confidence was issued, forcing Garland to resign almost immediately. He'd had enough anyway, if he was honest with himself. He knew he'd been stabbed in the back by a lot of ambitious people and knew he'd go down in history for the most deaths under his leadership since the Second World War. After a short vote (or was it short straw?) Conservative back-bencher Miles Livingstone was installed as the new Prime Minister, another Prime Minister not actually voted in by the general public. None of the top people in the cabinet wanted the job yet and were keeping their powder dry for better times before making their own leadership bid in the future. They all knew Miles Livingstone was just political cannon fodder - a stop-gap for now. The defenestration was complete, the metaphorical knives put away for another day. Britain was in crisis and confusion yet again. The British public didn't really care who was in charge as long as things improved and they all began to feel safe in their own homes again. The media challenged Livingstone to sort it all out very quickly. He was under massive pressure on his very first day in the job. He thought he would be able to survive and maybe solve the crisis quickly and become a national hero. The public were calling for a General Election but the noises from Westminster indicated that with the whole country in the midst of a crisis it really wasn't the right time to call one. It had only been just over two years since Garland had been installed as leader. Labour leader Nigel Wilkes-Scott was all for an election though, and he and his front bench MPs were spouting off their propaganda to the tabloids at every possible opportunity. They all jumped on the 'Mother Earth' bandwagon, promising to 'fix' the planet if the public would give them a chance. Of course, they were all hypocrites, driving around in big cars, flying all around the world for 'climate change' conferences. As ever, it was one rule for them and another for the general public trying to make ends meet in a country with spiralling inflation and taxation. At the moment the future looked bleak for almost everyone... whoever was in charge.

Vera Castle watched the latest news on her old TV. Well, that was unexpected, she thought. She didn't think the PM would suffer a vicious coup during a time of national emergency like this. She had no sympathy, of course, as the emergency was caused by her own doing based on his, and other world leaders, poor performance. Robert Garland's inaction over the last two years of his reign had helped to start her with her own actions and resort to the desperate measures she was forced into for the sake of the planet. She had actually thought about killing off a few world leaders to get her message across, hoping their replacements would be more willing to do something to avert the catastrophic climate change that was coming. Would that work? She supposed if she took credit for their deaths it would scare everyone enough to act but more likely it would delay things even more as the replacements tried to get to grips with the problems. She knew that if the elite were starting to be impacted then they would soon remove their collective fingers from their arseholes. Who would she choose first? She didn't like that American chap. Far too much of a rotten bully for her tastes. She then thought back to Gerald. Vera remembered how he had courted her and then dropped her when someone else came along. She had been devastated. Gerald had been her first and only boyfriend. She was a love-struck twentysomething in her final months of university. Gerald was a welcome distraction at a time when there was pressure to complete her degree. All work and no play and all that. He had romanced her at first. Candlelit dinners, walks in the park, the really good stuff. But he was getting frustrated because she wouldn't give in to his more amorous intentions. She wanted to wait - maybe until she was married to him. The situation caused arguments with Gerald. She hated that. She loved him. But did she love him that much? To just give in to him because he demanded it? She respected herself too much to cave in to him.

Eventually Gerald had cooled towards Vera. He called her less and less and the dinners and walks soon stopped too. She was worried it was the end, but thought she'd give him time to realise how much he loved and missed her and he would start to call again. She waited patiently for him. Several days later she was walking to a lecture and she saw Gerald sitting with a girl. She looked like a right slut and he was all over her like a cheap suit, pawing her in public and not caring who saw him. Gerald looked up from his disgusting behaviour and he saw Vera and smiled sheepishly. She knew it was over between them but he hadn't been man enough to actually tell her. What a bastard. She turned and fled in tears, missing the lecture and staying in her tiny bedsit alone for days, mostly crying her eyes out. No one noticed her absence. She wanted to hurt Gerald and she knew exactly how she would do it.

Tamanrasset, Southern Algeria.
August 7th.

Snow in August was almost unheard of anywhere outside of the two poles and it was very rare at any time in Africa at sea level. Tamanrasset, in Southern Algeria, was a Saharan oasis town, mainly known for fruit production; dates, figs and citrus fruits primarily, also some cereals. Dotted around outside of the town, in the desert, were strange rock formations caused by erosion from the harsh Saharan winds. Life in Tamanrasset hadn't changed much in two hundred years. Life had gone on as usual.

Fatin Mouhandiz was busy picking figs as it was time to harvest. Once picked they would be dried in the sun and then transported to Algiers and then on to the European market. His two sons, Ahmed and Omar, were also working on the harvest while his wife, Basira was tending to things in their small farmhouse on the outskirts of the town.

The first flakes floated down from a sunny sky. There were no clouds where they could come from. Fatin looked up in amazement. He'd never seen snow in his lifetime other than once in a film when he took his family to Algiers to visit family who were lucky enough to have a television. He asked Allah what was happening and if he was being punished for something. Fatin shouted to the two small boys to stop and run to the small hand cart he used to move the figs to the drying area near his home. The sons immediately complied and were sitting in the cart when Fatin got to it. He pushed with all his strength, all the time praying to his God to spare him and the boys.

It was hard work pushing the cart with the two children in, both now crying in fear. Snow was falling more heavily now and the thin wheels of the cart had made narrow tracks in the snow behind him. He had never felt such cold in his life and together with the confusion and panic his mind wandered. He became lethargic and the cart slowed. The snow continued to fall and soon reached over six feet in height. Hundreds died from suffocation, trapped in the ever increasing snow drifts long before hypothermia could take them. The town virtually died that day. Not only was there a large loss of life but all the crops were destroyed by the snow. The survivors moved away from Tamanrasset, most leaving whatever belongings they had behind because it was easier to move on foot without carrying any bulky bundles. Basira wept as she walked as part of the long column moving from the town. She knew there had been no hope for her husband and sons and prayed that their bodies would eventually be found when the snows disappeared.

London.
August 9th

Steve had got a taxi to Pete's house to pick up Jane for their date as she had taken the day off work and spent it with her sister. He'd been thinking about Garland resigning and thought that Karma had been at work again, although he wouldn't have wanted the Wembley tragedy to be the catalyst, of course. Garland was an arrogant dickhead, but was he really responsible for what was happening? If he was, then all the world leaders should be forced to resign, especially that dodgy effeminate bloke in Canada. He pushed that thought from his mind and focused on the evening's date with Jane. He had booked the restaurant early that morning. A nice cosy Italian place called Giorgio's. Jane was ready for him when he arrived and Pete stood at the door waving and shouting "Don't be back too late, kids." Steve's middle digit rose in response to him. The ride lasted six or seven minutes before the taxi rolled up outside the restaurant in a quiet back street. Steve paid the driver and rushed around to open the door for Jane. He ushered her inside and was met by a swarthy looking waiter with a huge moustache who showed them to their small table in the corner and then lit the candle in a silver holder in the middle of the lacy white tablecloth and then slunk off to get a couple of menus for them. The restaurant wasn't too busy, just another two couples in the place, so the only real noise was the subtle classical music and the clinking of plates and cutlery coming from behind the double swing doors leading out to the kitchen. The waiter came back with the menus and a wine list. They settled for the house white and then Steve ordered his favourite Italian dish: Grilled calamari, rocket and chillies topped with olive oil and lovely creamy mash. Jane took a little longer to decide, she admitted she was quite unfamiliar when it came to Italian food and had trouble choosing - it all looked good to her. Her procrastination was making the waiter visibly irritated, but finally she settled for Sicilian red prawn Carpaccio with fennel, orange and large black olives. While they waited for the food there was the usual small talk - jobs, hobbies and interests, until the dishes arrived and they ate mainly in silence, apart from the exaggerated 'mmmm' from them both. Desserts were ordered, delivered and consumed. Tiramisu for Steve and Lemon Pannacotta topped with blueberries for his lovely date. In between bites, Steve looked up and loved how Jane looked. At Pete's the other evening she was casually dressed in jeans and sweatshirt but she had really made the effort for their date and that made Steve feel a bit honoured that she'd made herself up to look this nice just for him. It was a good evening, good food, good conversation and a lot of good laughs. Was he falling for her? He hadn't even liked his ex-wife this much, even when they were together, especially before they were married. Could Jane really be 'the one' this time? He was fairly sure he wasn't ready for all that yet. He wanted to take things slowly at first and see how things panned out for them.

The meal was over but they sat there talking over multiple cups of sweet black coffee and glasses of the expensive brandy on the wine list. It was the best evening he could remember for a long time. Jane felt the same. After a few abusive boyfriends over the years it was great to find a guy who seemed to be nice and genuine. He was polite and treated her with respect too, which was unusual in this day and age. He was a few years older than her but she liked that. Quite mature and reserved. He was from a different era. One that treated women a lot better than men did now. She really liked him and the fact that her sister had said a lot of good things, luckily more good than bad, about Steve had convinced her to take a chance and go on the date. She really didn't need her sister's recommendation really as she had already been impressed with him when they had drinks and the takeaway at Pete and Jackie's house a few nights ago, but her sister's thoughts had just confirmed what she herself had thought about him. She hadn't felt this comfortable with anyone for years. She knew she'd developed a wariness when it came to men but she felt totally at ease with Steve. She knew it was a bit early to think of a future with him after just one date and drinks the other night, but thought this time, just maybe, it would all work out for her and she'd finally be happy for the first time in her life. She just got a vibe from him that everything would be alright for them. She smiled inwardly at that thought and outwardly as Steve told her a few embarrassing stories about Pete that even her own sister didn't know about... and hoped she'd never find out.

They finally took the hint from the impatient waiter constantly yawning and willing them to leave the restaurant. They had been the only customers left for at least forty minutes but they both didn't want the evening to end. Steve paid the bill, refusing Jane's offer to go dutch. That impressed her too. She knew that a modern man probably expected her to go halves on the meal. She was not a rampant feminist, so thought it was nice of him to insist and said she'd pay next time. Next time? She admitted to herself that there would be a next time. She liked the old values and thought she was probably born in the wrong era. She would have felt right at home in the forties or fifties. Even though people lived through a war and then were under the threat of a nuclear holocaust afterwards, she thought people were a lot happier in general back then. There was still rationing and bomb sites all over London but they all coped well and they stuck together and supported each other. Now it seemed to be everyone was out for themselves and the majority of people seemed very selfish. Steve was definitely not selfish although at times he was a bit guarded about his past, especially his failed marriage, but to be honest she didn't really expect him to open up about *everything* on a first date. But she still wanted to know more about him and would be happy to make this a regular thing. Get to know each other properly with no pressure on either of them. Whatever happened between them she wanted to at least stay friends with Steve. He was pretty unique in her eyes.

They left the restaurant and walked a short distance down the dark, deserted street to a taxi rank. Steve thought he should have called for a cab while they were still inside but the weather was nice and they were happy to walk a couple of hundred yards. He thought about putting his arm around her but was worried he'd be rejected and that would spoil a very pleasant evening. He settled for holding her hand as they walked. Jane smiled up at him sweetly. They reached the taxi rank and headed for the front of the queue of four cars and got into the back of a black Mercedes C Class. The driver took them the four miles to Jane's flat and waited a few minutes for Steve to say goodbye at the doorstep. Steve wasn't the kind of guy who expected to be invited in after a first date. Jane did think about ushering him in through the front door and was both relieved and a little disappointed Steve didn't suggest staying the night. He went up a few more notches in her estimation for that. She did hug him and kiss him on the cheek after thanking him for a brilliant evening. Steve was still smiling as he got back in the rear of the cab and they travelled onward towards his own place. He was grateful the driver wasn't too talkative. He was happily immersed with his own thoughts about Jane and the excellent evening they'd had. He finally arrived home to a dark and empty flat, poured himself a large scotch and sat in his big leather chair, deep in thought. He finally dozed off in the chair, the empty crystal glass fell from his hand into his lap.

Steve was in a park somewhere, he wasn't sure where exactly, the skyline looked like London, but it could have been any city in England. How did he get here? Where was he going? Dusk was beginning to fall and he was getting quite nervous. Feral gangs were rife in London and other cities these days, but was he actually in London? He had no idea. Nothing looked very familiar to him but he had never strayed too much from the areas his flat or studio were in and he usually travelled within walking distance. If he went slightly further afield he usually jumped on a bus or a tube train and just switched off from everything, listening to the tunes on his MP3 player, until he got to his destination. Is that what happened? He didn't remember getting on any transport, though. He checked his pocket for his wallet. Empty! No money. How the hell would he get home? Phone Pete? He looked in his other pocket. No bloody phone. Had he been mugged and been wandering around in a daze for hours? He felt fine, no aches and pains. He cautiously wiped his hands across his face. No blood or even sweat evident. What the hell had happened? It was definitely getting darker. He had to find a phone box to call Pete and ask to reverse the charges. He walked on a little further and reached the edge of the park. He spotted a lone phone booth in the distance and headed towards it. It seemed to take ages to get there, longer than it should. Why was he walking so slowly? His peripheral vision was very blurred and his surroundings only came into focus when he turned his head. Did he have concussion? He realised he hadn't seen anyone else in the park. Had there been another event orchestrated by Mother Earth? Had everyone been evacuated except for him, or was he a lone survivor? Nothing made much sense to him at the moment. What had happened to make him wander through this park, and presumably the streets alone? He finally reached the phone box. Fucking vandalised. What a surprise. He carried on in the hope of finding a working phone or even someone who would be kind enough to let him use theirs. Shame most people were total arseholes and wouldn't even piss on you if you were on fire these days. Thank Christ he wasn't on fire because the streets were deserted. Things, and people, had changed so much since he was a kid, he thought sadly. All of the shops were closed. Nothing to be seen through their windows but darkness inside. It was almost fully dark outside now and he began to hear a rustling in the trees to his left. What time was it? He didn't wear a watch and just used his missing phone to tell him the time. He was now desperate to find a working phone. Pete would be here like a shot... wherever here was. He wasn't sure Pete would ever find him. The area was very quiet apart from some faint squeaks, like a child riding around on a rusty bicycle, but could see nothing. Strangely he couldn't smell anything either. Then everything erupted all around him. A swarm of large bats flew from the nearby trees. He didn't even think bats lived in trees. Where was the nearest belfry anyway? They flew over him and he ducked sharply and tried to make his way to a dark doorway in the street, crouch walking like Groucho Marx. His stance grew lower and lower as the bats repeatedly buzzed him. He got to the doorway and pulled himself as close to the crumbling red brickwork as he could. Then he realised he had become cornered and helpless. He battered at the door, flaking green paint floated slowly to the ground. The bats hit him almost as one solid body of wings, teeth and fur. Steve screamed. The bats nipped him with their sharp fangs, they mercilessly clawed at him too. A couple of them were tangled in his hair and thrashing about, pulling his hair out by the roots. This is it, he thought. The bats burrowed deeper into him.

Steve jolted awake. He wasn't sure if he had screamed out or not, but it was very possible. He was thankful it had only been a bad dream. It seemed so real though. He hurriedly checked his hair for the bats and his face and hands for bites and scratches. Nothing. Christ, he hated those creepy little buggers at the best of times. It was as if someone had delved into his head and found one of his biggest fears and projected the scenario into his mind. That was just stupid, of course. No one could do that. He thought about making himself another drink but decided against it. Coffee was definitely out of the question as he had to be up fairly early. He pushed himself up from his comfy chair that he had slept in on many occasions and stopped off at the toilet before falling flatly on top of his bed. He didn't even bother taking his clothes off although he did managed to unlace his shoes and slip them off before rolling into a fetal position, hoping there would be no continuation of that dream. Luckily, he slept soundly for the rest of the night.

Steve awoke the next morning at just after seven, slightly dehydrated as his mobile rang its annoying default ring tone - he'd need to change that, maybe find a sample of AC/DC or Thin Lizzy. He'd only had the phone just over a week and hadn't had time to change it yet. Why were the pre-installed ring tones and alarms so bloody annoying? And everyone used the same three or four. When someone's phone rang everyone else checked theirs, sometimes it was quite comical to witness. It was a bit like the school bell at the end of the day, he remembered - everyone reacting to the same thing at that very moment. Was that called 'herd mentality? He wasn't really sure.

It was Pete on the phone asking Steve how the evening had gone. The first question was "Where are you?"

"I'm at home - thanks for waking me, mate. The alarm was set for another hour, you dick. Why are you up at sparrow fart? It's not like you!" said Steve as he walked to the kitchen to first have a drink of water and then fill the kettle, putting his phone on speaker so he could use both hands.

"Jackie has been digging me in the ribs for half an hour to find out how things went last night," laughed Pete.

"Why couldn't she have called Jane herself?"

"She didn't want to wake her up, mate," said Pete sheepishly, knowing he'd get a backlash from Steve.

"Oh, so it's fine to wake me then!" growled Steve.

"Sorry, but you know what she's like - all she could talk about last night was how it could be going. Ruined the bloody film we were watching. So how did it go? Good times?"

"Yes, we had a very pleasant evening, the food was excellent and the conversation was even better. I dropped her off and came back here and crashed out with a large scotch," said Steve. Getting slightly irritated at the grilling Pete was having to do on behalf of Jackie.

"Sounds like you were a complete gentleman, didn't you fancy her or what?"

"Of course I do, but during the evening I realised that she was a bit special and I didn't want to blow things by coming on too strong."

"Fair enough mate, Jackie was a bit worried you'd get drunk and jump her," chuckled Pete.

"Well, thank Jackie for her concern and tell her that I behaved impeccably, I like Jane a lot," replied Steve.

"Good to hear and you really don't want Jackie kicking your arse if you misbehave, do you?" said Pete.

"Like she kicks your arse then? No need to worry on that score, Pete, I should give Jane a call and thank her again and maybe arrange another date. Maybe a day out somewhere. Hampton Court? Tower of London? Somewhere like that," said Steve.

"Good idea, Maybe even Hastings, or Battle, to be precise, we did love it there. They sell mead in the gift shop, which is quite nice. Dover Castle is good too."

"I'll get on the internet and do some research. Our school did a trip to Battle when I was a kid, but I missed it because I got chickenpox. All my mates loved it while I was at home in bed scratching myself stupid," sighed Steve.

"That's got to be a pisser, especially at that age. Anyway - that's a good reason to take Jane now - make up for your childhood loss and have a great day out with her too, double bubble, mate."

"I'm convinced. I'll ring her and see what she says. Maybe she won't want another date?" said Steve, now having doubts.

"I don't think you have to worry on that score, mate. From what she was saying to Jackie and me after you went home after the drinks and takeaway she seemed pretty keen, although she doesn't want to be too forward. She wants to take thing a little slower than in the past and that, my old friend, is a very good sign in my considered opinion. It seems neither of you want to mess things up with each other, so stay cool and take your time. Become friends before anything else, mate, and you'll both be fine. You can thank your old uncle Pete at the wedding," laughed Pete.

"Don't go suggesting that to Jackie, for feck's sake. You know, you could get a job as a newspaper agony aunt. Do they even still have them, or do people just screw up their lives without any kind of advice now? I *will* take things slowly, though. You know I like her, and even after only meeting her twice I know I want her in my life, even as just a friend, but more would be brilliant. She's a lovely girl."

"You know me and Jackie want the same for you both, Steve. Anyway, I'll let you get yourself sorted for the day and I'll see you at the office a bit later. I should be there about two. Jackie wants me to take her shopping. Probably for a hat for the wedding, ha, ha!"

"Piss off, you dick," said Steve, grinning and hung up.

Steve looked at the kitchen clock and saw it was almost seven-thirty. He wasn't sure if Jane would be working today and getting ready, or even commuting, but decided to take the chance. He pulled up her mobile number from his contacts list and pressed the little green phone icon. The phone rang twice in his ear and she answered. Steve was relieved.

"Hi, Steve. How are you doing this morning?" Steve could tell from her voice she was smiling. A good start.

"I feel good apart from Pete ringing a bit earlier to find out how things went. Jackie bullied him into calling me instead of you. I really enjoyed last night, Jane," he said.

"So did I. It was really nice. Great place to eat, not too busy either. I didn't realise we were the last to leave. I was probably too engrossed in the conversation to notice," she said.

"I was the same until I noticed the waiter yawning and the barman leaning on the bar trying his best not to look put out. Then we left about half an hour later," Steve laughed. "So-"

"So-" Jane said at the exact same moment. They both laughed. "You first," said Steve.

"So, I was thinking that we could maybe do it again? Maybe make a day of it? What do you think?" she asked.

"Exactly what I was going to ask, great minds and all that," he laughed.

"We do seem to have a connection, Steve. I really like that."

"I think you're right... we're right," he replied. Anyway, you have a think about where to go, Pete and I came up with a few possibilities but I'd like to know what you think. It would be weird if we did come up with a list of the same places, prove that connection again."

"Yes, it really would be strange. I'll definitely have a think about where we could go but I'm happy to go anywhere really, I'm sure we'll make it a fun day of it wherever we are. I assume you want to avoid weekends because of the crowds?

I'm not keen on a lot of people around me either and during the week would be much nicer," she said.

"Suits me perfectly, I'll talk to you soon, and thanks again for last night. I need to get ready to set things up for the podcast later, so bye for now, Jane."

They both ended the call but wishing they could have talked for a bit longer. Happiness mixed with a little sadness for both but they knew there would be plenty of time for talking on the next date if they would be together all day.

Gloucester, England.
August 11th.

Vera Castle decided to do a little shopping in Gloucester before her shift at GCHQ started at noon. She rarely ventured into the city but she had to visit the bank instead of doing her usual thing with them online. Vera hated mixing with people and the crowded city was a nightmare for her. The hustle and bustle of a town or city always made her nervous, if not close to panicking. After finishing at the bank she picked up a few bits and pieces from Wilko and Poundstretchers and was making her way back to the car park when a fast food delivery rider almost ran her over with his electric bike. She fumed. She'd get her revenge but she'd wait until the idiot was a couple of hundred yards away to avoid any suspicion falling on her. She had to be very careful, especially now. She didn't want anyone suspecting her of being Mother Earth and disrupting or delaying her plans.

Vojin Maric was an illegal immigrant from Serbia and had been in the UK for over ten years. He'd bought a French passport from an Albanian criminal gang two years previously and now worked as a Deliveroo employee, rushing around on the brand new electric bike he'd bought a few weeks ago. It had replaced the battered old mountain bike he'd stolen and repainted and now it meant he could do many more pick-ups and deliveries because the electric bike was faster and he never got tired either. He had a pretty nice life now and rented a small furnished flat over a charity shop in the centre of Gloucester. It was much better than sharing with the several other illegals like he did for a few years. He wished he had been one of those illegals put up for free in four star hotels all around the country but he arrived long before the British government started to do that. He was finally happy after years of looking over his shoulder and worrying about being deported back to Novi Sad. At least he could work now.

He enjoyed his job and also bumping into the other riders he knew when he was picking up from a McDonalds, KFC or Starbucks. The harder he worked, the more money he made and that suited him perfectly. He was friends on social media with a few girls from his home city and maybe one day he could bring one over to live with him, hopefully Jelena, a beautiful dark-haired girl who worked in a pharmacy there. He had no family left to bring over after the terrible war with Croatia, both older brothers were killed in the fighting and his parents dying before the war even started when he was little more than a baby. After several years in an orphanage he decided to try and make a better life for himself in Western Europe. He finally got to France and risked his life to cross the English Channel in a small rubber boat with about a dozen others after paying the people smugglers all he had saved by doing odd jobs on his journey from Novi Sad through to Calais.

As he rushed towards Nandos for a pick up on the mainly pedestrianised High Street, he almost hit a large woman with his bike. He looked back towards her apologetically and saw she was staring intensely at him. He thought nothing of it and carried on towards the restaurant. Then he started to feel some heat coming from the seat of the bike. He looked down and saw a small, thin wisp of grey smoke coming from beneath the seat where the battery was stored. He was beginning to slow down to get off and have a proper look when the seat burst into flames, igniting the black polyester jogging bottoms he was wearing. He screamed at the intense pain as the trousers melted and stuck to his thighs and genitals. He tried to beat at the flames as they spread to his shirt and then lost control of the bike which ploughed straight through the glass front of a Subway store, scattering all the people queued for their sandwiches. It took Vojin several minutes to die horribly on the floor of the fast food shop he had visited many times over the last few years. The pain from the burns had been incredible. When the ambulance finally arrived it was way too late and he became a takeaway himself.

Vera had watched all the commotion from afar as she had done with a lot of her victims over the last couple of decades. She knew that no one would ever get away with upsetting her for long, just like Gerald. Retribution was usually swift for these idiots all around her. She did contemplate trying to give someone cancer so her revenge would take a lot longer and be more painful for the victim but found it took too much of her energy to do it. She would get very exhausted. Her vengeance always had to be short and sweet. Disappointing, but necessary for her own health. She needed to be fully fit, both physically and especially mentally, for the work she had to do to save the planet.

Kent, England.
August 13th.

Steve had rented a car for the day - only a small automatic Mercedes A Class but it was surprising nippy and handled the motorway on the way down to Dover pretty well. He'd picked Jane up from her place around ten a.m. after picking the car up from the rental company which was within walking distance from his home. He'd originally pre-booked a Ford Fiesta type for two days but the man in the car hire office offered him an upgrade for the same price which he was quite happy with. He didn't really like Fords too much anyway and initially reserving something better like the Merc would have been another hundred quid.

On the journey down they talked, and talked... and talked. Every subject was interesting, nothing seemed boring to them. But they talked about music mainly while a collection of rock songs was playing at a low volume streamed from Steve's phone to the car stereo. It turned out that Jane was as big a fan of classic rock as Steve was and even sang along to some of the tunes. It was a great start to the day on a usually tedious trip along the busy motorway. Then Steel Panther came on the stereo with one of their explicit, but fun, songs. Steve got slightly embarrassed but Jane went into hysterical laughter at the lyrics. Asian Hooker was a big hit with her and she vowed to check out all their stuff on Youtube. Steve had recently discovered Steel Panther after they were mentioned in one of Mark Mason's books.

They talked more and they laughed. It was going to be a brilliant day out, thought Steve. He hoped the weather would hold up for the day. They reached Dover Castle but were directed to the overflow car park about a mile away. A regular coach shuttle was provided from the car park to the castle but they decided to walk down the hill instead, a bit of alone time before the small crowds Steve expected at the castle itself. Steve paid for them both to enter the grounds and they made their way through the large gate in the outer wall and into the main enclosure. As Steve had thought, the crowd wasn't too bad. Quite bearable, in fact. Coming on a weekday was a good idea. He'd hate to see how many people would be there on a weekend. Parking would be a nightmare. A lot more kids would be running around and being far too noisy too. Jane suggested getting a coffee and something to eat before they started, so she bought an Americano and a pastry each for them and they sat at an outdoor bench and table while they watched all the comings and goings of the people at the castle. It was a lovely day which probably meant a slightly bigger crowd than usual, hence the overflow car park being used. Not ideal but they would take things at their own pace and if a certain part of the site was too busy they would go back to it later. She was sure others would arrive a bit later.

When the lovely, strong coffee was finished, they walked leisurely around the various, and interesting, exhibits. Steve particularly liked the displays of all the uniforms of the regiments who had been stationed at the castle over the years. There were lots of weapons from different eras on show too going way back to the 11th or 12th Century.

Jane really loved the exhibit and the story of Eleanor of Aquitane, the wife of Henry II. She had encouraged her two sons, Henry and Richard to rebel and overthrow the king.

They wanted to tour the magnificent keep last so next they visited the Saxon church. On the walk they were talking about Saxons and Jane couldn't resist banging out "Wheeeels, Wheels of Steel," at the top of her voice, getting strange looks from most people around apart from a long haired biker who nodded appreciatively and smiled. Steve gave her a mock disgusted look and then grinned at her. She's too bloody perfect, he thought. Beautiful and a Saxon fan on top. Was she his Princess of the Night?

They finally made it to the keep a little later in the day, a fairly tall almost rectangular structure in the centre of the site. It was very cool inside compared to the fairly warm sun outside. They both found it very interesting - a reconstructed medieval kitchen was on the ground floor, fake food on the tables and in cooking pots for effect. On the higher floors they particularly liked the armoury and the King's bed chamber. Jane wondered what it would have been like to have lived there in those times - probably a bit cold. They both took a lot of pictures on their phones. The best part was a play that was being put on. King Henry II was ranting wildly at his minions. Steve thought it was quite funny. There were maybe fifty other tourists crammed around the chamber to witness the colourful spectacle. 'Henry' was obviously enjoying playing up to the crowd and probably grinned more than the real Henry had his whole life. If Pete was there he would have likened the royal rant as part of working in a modern day call centre. Steve thought that the real Henry would have been a bit of an obnoxious bully. No wonder his wife wanted her two sons to bump him off and take power. She could have been the first Queen of all England, although by proxy. There was no doubt she would have been calling the shots behind the scenes.

They found their way up to the flat roof of the keep. There was a spectacular view of the Kent countryside on one side and the English Channel on the other. Steve could see where he had parked the black Mercedes in the overflow car park. It was a lovely clear sunny day and they could see for miles. There was no trace of any wind to give them a chill, even that high up, it was certainly warmer than inside, Steve thought. They stayed up there for almost ten minutes before the sky started to darken slightly. Steve thought that a bit of un-forecasted rain wouldn't ruin the day too much as they had had a great time so far and would cram themselves into one of the coffee shops along with everyone else if it poured down or maybe take the shuttle bus back to the car and find somewhere else to visit in Dover itself. He noticed it was still lovely and calm out to sea though. There were a good many small boats out on the water. Some were just white specks in the distance, but a few nearer ones having to use their motors because of the lack of wind out there.

Steve then turned around and couldn't believe what he saw. A dark grey rotating spout was heading towards the castle from the direction of the countryside. A tornado in Britain? They were very rare but nothing like the size of the thing heading towards them. Steve didn't panic, though. He calmly grabbed Jane's arm and pulled her quickly towards the entrance to the roof. Others were not quite so vigilant or swift to react as quickly as Steve did. As the giant tornado hit, Steve had managed to drag Jane through the opening and down the flight of cold worn stone steps to safety where they huddled together on a landing waiting for the others to follow. No one did. Those still on the roof were swept up in the dark plume of wind and debris. Some were flung out to sea, broken bones or unconsciousness meaning they drowned very quickly. Some were thrown against the stone walls of the castle and the church. Steve closed his eyes at the sound of the screams, just thankful that he and Jane had made it off the roof to relative safety in time. He silently prayed the main structure would hold up to the onslaught of freak weather.

The tornado disappeared just as quickly as it had arrived. When the wind had died down there was an eerie silence for several minutes as those who had survived tried in vain to process what had happened to them. The people inside the great tower had been the lucky ones. Most of those outside were either gone or lying in untidy heaps, broken beyond all recognition. Pools of blood and body parts were all around the courtyard. Steve told Jane to stay where she was and he tentatively climbed the steps again to see if anyone else from the roof had survived. The flat roof was deserted as he had expected though. Not a trace of a single soul, apart from a smashed Nikon camera lying close to the parapet. He warily inched closer to the edge. The tower had fortunately remained intact which showed how well it was built more than eight-hundred years before. He looked out into the distance. The overflow car park had totally gone - as well as all of the cars. Steve's first thought was 'bugger me!' His second was how much excess he'd be paying on the insurance for the car even though it was rented. Christ! These rental companies screw you for even a tiny scratch, he thought.

Steve made his way back to the roof's exit and quickly down the steps. Jane was still there, now on her feet, with her back to the wall and quite close to tears. He gave her a hug, thankful they had both survived. He realised he dreaded losing her. As they made their way down through the multiple levels they witnessed the shock in all the other survivors, those who, through either luck or fate, were inside the massive structure when the tornado hit. Some were in tears, some in hysterics and some just looked stunned by the experience, almost catatonic. There were others, though, who looked quite stoic and possibly used to a crisis going on around them and they were trying to calm down the most upset people in the group. 'King Henry' sat on his throne with his head held in his hands. His fake golden crown had fallen off and lay upside down on the red carpet in front of him. Others had scrambled to the windows to look at the devastation outside between the keep and the castle walls, all fighting for a good view, phones and cameras ready for a good shot at the damage, and especially the carnage. Steve didn't know what to do. Stay there or make their way outside? He could hear several sirens in the distance, all getting louder by the second. Help was on the way, although Steve wasn't sure what help they could actually give apart from handing out a sedative to half the survivors in the keep. 'Henry' certainly looked like he needed something. Steve realised he could do with a large scotch or three. Jane was still clinging tightly to him, still not sure if it was all real or some sort of bad dream. Steve put his arms around her and told her that they had survived and would be fine and just had to keep calm and wait for the emergency services to take charge of the terrible situation. She lightly rested her head on his shoulder. He expected tears from her but they didn't come, maybe they would later when they were well away from this disaster area. Then Steve wondered how the hell they were going to get home with the rental car gone.

The emergency services did the best they could in the appallingly difficult circumstances. Although well trained in disaster management they had never had to deal with a tornado before and the protocols they worked to had to be quickly adapted to the current situation. It was more like the scene of a terrible terrorist bombing than anything else. Steve and Jane were both ushered to a police incident tent set up just outside the outer walls where they were asked to give a short statement about who they were, where they were when the disaster happened, and what they were doing. Initial reports of terrorism at the castle were soon dismissed as the police talked to the survivors who all gave the same story of the massive tornado. This seemed to be yet another 'natural' event. Steve was already forming the next podcast in his head. This was the second time he had barely escaped one of these things after the incident at the BBC studios in London a few weeks ago. Did Mother Earth have it in for him? He was a hundred percent sure this had been her doing.

The police had laid on minibuses to get the survivors to Dover Station as all of them had lost the transport they had arrived in. They were told to pay for the tickets home themselves and they would be compensated for the cost... eventually. They arrived at Dover Priory Station with a small group of shocked survivors, bought tickets for the next available train, and patiently waited. Steve was relieved he'd be getting the ticket money back. A hundred quid for the pair of them to St. Pancras! Daylight robbery! The last time he'd been on a train it was thirty-five pounds for a return to Birmingham to visit a friend for the day. Certainly better times for a lot of reasons. There was a cheaper way going to London Victoria, still forty pounds but the journey took twice as long and had a long wait before they could board and they wanted to get back as soon as possible and the promise of getting the fare back made the decision a bit easier. They wanted to try and get a bit of normality back. All through the hour and ten minute journey they both just stared in silence out of the window as the train sped across the Kent countryside towards London. Steve held Jane's hand and gave it the odd squeeze but he thought she didn't really seem to notice the comforting contact. When they arrived at St. Pancras, Jane suggested they got a taxi to her place as it was nearer than Steve's. Steve was happy with that. He didn't really want to be alone and neither did he want Jane to be on her own for a while.

They got back to her flat and sat on the sofa snuggled up together. Eventually, she put on the TV news and they were glued to the coverage on the large screen. The camera crews hadn't arrived by the time Steve and Jane had left but there was now plenty of drone footage of the castle which luckily meant the blood and body parts strewn around the grounds were virtually impossible to make out from the rest of the general rubble at the site. The Sky reporter's piece to camera from outside the walls was much sensationalised, as usual, in Steve's opinion, but what did you expect now? Apparently according to 'witness reports' a tornado had appeared out of nowhere, a fact confirmed by the Met Office and nearby RAF bases. Nothing had shown up on radar until the freak thing struck and then disappeared off the screens just as rapidly. Sky brought on their usual 'experts' who were completely clueless about the events. They did say that Britain sometimes experienced the odd small tornado every few years but they did very little damage and happened mostly on farmland. It was even rarer that a populated area had been the site of one of the small ones but this large tornado was both unexpected and truly devastating. Initial reports said the death toll was over three hundred, although even a rough number was difficult due to the condition of the bodies, while just under a hundred and forty people inside the tower and in the wartime tunnels had survived. They said it could take many months before a true figure could be ascertained and that would be through DNA analysis and the resulting investigation. It was another grim day for Britain, which seemed to be hit by these disasters a lot more frequently than other countries. Was that significant? The experts mused over all sorts of theories, including the work of Mother Earth. Was Mother Earth operating from Britain - it certainly seemed like it. Maybe she, or they, were targeting places they knew or had visited?

Pete had called to make sure they were both alright after their ordeal and professed his guilt at suggesting the castle as a day out. Steve told him not to be an idiot and to get drunk or something to take his mind off it. Steve then told Pete that they needed to get into the office early in the morning and plan the next broadcast for the afternoon. Strike while the iron was hot with another of his eyewitness accounts. Pete agreed, told him to make sure Jane was okay, and they said goodnight.

Jane ordered a large pizza for them both at around nine o'clock and forty minutes later it arrived but they both sat picking at it. Neither were that hungry even though it was Steve's favourite; pepperoni with pineapple and chillies. Eventually they turned off the TV as everything was just being repeated ad nauseam and nothing new was coming to light from Dover. It was too depressing for them both and realised they had been incredibly fortunate to have survived. They sat quietly in the dark and dozed, each embroiled in their private thoughts of their lucky escape. If Steve had suffered from paranoia he would have thought that, after two near misses, Mother Earth was out to get him.

He was on top of the keep, all alone on the roof. The place was quiet and peaceful and the view was very serene. Why was he alone though? Where the hell was Jane? His phone rang and he fished it out of the front pocket of his jeans and looked at the name on the screen. It was Pete. Pete's voice sounded a bit strange as if he was far away in a long tunnel, there was lots of echo and a bit of hissing in the background. It sounded like Pete was trying to warn him about something but he couldn't understand exactly what it was. Steve kept shouting to his friend that he had to talk more slowly and a bit clearer. What was Pete going on about? It wasn't like Pete to sound so scared of something, whatever it might be, even Jackie. Steve was getting very frustrated and a little bit nervous. The sky grew ever darker. Surely Pete wouldn't be bothering to warn him about a bit of rain, which was stupid to be scared about, wasn't it? Maybe it was a thunderstorm? The roof of the tall keep was probably not the best place to be if there was a risk of lightning. The badly burnt image of Dan French shot back into his mind although the police never showed any pictures. He decided he needed to get off the roof quickly, back to the safety of the keep. He walked fairly swiftly towards the entrance to the roof, trying to stay calm. There was a large oak door with iron rivets and plates to strengthen it. Was that there when he had arrived on the roof a few minutes ago? It certainly wasn't closed, he knew that for sure. Steve tried hard to push it open. It didn't budge and then thought it was more than likely to open outward so he tugged at the cold, black iron handle. Still nothing. It was shut tightly. The door didn't even rattle in its frame as he pushed, pulled and even kicked at the door. It was solid. It was then he started to panic. He shouted loudly for Jane to help him open the door then screamed at anyone who may be on the other side of the obstruction. He was pleading for assistance, terrified of being alone and the danger a thunderstorm could bring. He heard a distant rumble. Shit! It was beginning to start. He looked around for somewhere that would shield him from the coming storm. He didn't mind getting wet but being struck by lightning was a hell of a lot worse. There was nowhere obvious to hide himself. Steve was getting increasingly anxious now. He knew he could be in serious trouble. Maybe even fatally. The image of Dan's smouldering body popped into his head again. Shit!! Steve moved to each of the four sides of the cold stone parapet, looking for a way down. No ladders or a fire escape there - he was trapped on the roof. Obviously jumping wasn't an option, even if there was soft grass all around the building - it was way too high. Ninety or almost a hundred feet he seemed to remember when he researched the trip. There wasn't any grass near to the keep anyway. The ground was cobbled all around the building. He'd break every bone in his body if he was stupid enough to try and leap to safety. Think, Steve, he told himself. Bloody think! There must be something he could do. He always believed there was a solution to any problem except death, of course, and if he didn't come up with something very soon he may be facing that ultimate journey. He ran across the roof and tried the solid, wooden door again. Maybe his previous shouting had attracted someone's attention on the staircase so shouted to anyone on the other side again. Still nothing - no help. He turned around, resting his back on the cold, oak door then started to slide down so he was sitting on the chilled flagstones which made up the roof. Then he saw it. It wasn't a storm with potentially fatal lightning after all. It was something much, much worse. Surely it wasn't possible. Not in bloody Kent! A huge tornado was heading menacingly towards the castle. It seemed to bring back a memory from somewhere or something in his brain. He stared at the dark conical plume for what seemed like an eternity, totally numb. He was frozen there. What the hell could he do? He knew from films like Twister that tornadoes were massively destructive and usually fatal for those caught in their path. The frightening rumble grew even louder and the dark grey funnel got ever nearer, starting to fill the whole sky before him. The sound was really deafening now, making it almost impossible for Steve to think. His last thought was not for himself. He wondered where Jane was and if she was safe. He realised he probably loved her and felt incredibly sad that he'd probably never see her again. He decided to lie flat on his stomach and try and grip the icy cold flagstones with his bare fingers as best he could. He knew it would probably make no difference in the end. He felt this was the end - his end. The tornado would undoubtedly demolish the tower anyway and his broken and bloody body would be found in the rubble afterwards by rescue workers. He could hear the tornado start to howl violently but he was too terrified to look up at it. He closed his eyes tightly and waited for the inevitable. He started to feel a sensation of being weightless. Then he was whisked up into the spinning vortex, a mixture of small and large pieces of debris constantly hitting him, breaking his bones. Strangely there was very little pain. And then he was flung out of the dark funnel and falling... falling-

Steve woke very suddenly. He hadn't screamed. At least he didn't think so, or the silent naked form of Jane beside him would have been startled awake too. Shit - it was just another bad dream. He was sweating and panting but he was still alive and in one piece. He remembered then that he was at Jane's place because they went there after what happened to them at Dover Castle as it was nearer the station. He slowly got up from the double bed, using his hand on the papered wall to navigate to the bedroom door, feeling his fingertips slide lightly over the embossed pattern. He found the bedroom door and slowly opened it in case it creaked loudly and woke Jane. Steve found his way through to the kitchen and then quickly rinsed the scotch glass he'd found on the small coffee table as he passed through the quiet living room. He filled the glass at the kitchen sink and tried to control his breathing and heart rate by sipping slowly at the cold water and staring out of the window, trying to keep his mind blank. There was no lighting outside so all he saw was his topless reflection staring back at him with hollow, haunted eyes and spiky bed hair. After a few minutes he had calmed down enough to try and recall the dream while picking at the dried out pizza still in its greasy box on the kitchen counter. It had felt so real. He was alone, on the roof of the keep and then caught up in the tornado. He hadn't had such a vivid dream since he was about seven and knew he had to urinate on a crocodile in a big rubber paddling pool in order to kill it. Then he'd discovered he had wet the bed and started to cry. Thank God he never needed to piss on anything in that dream tonight. Not with Jane sleeping next to him. That would have put a real dampener on their new relationship... literally. He sipped some more water and then crept his way back into the bedroom and checked the sheet for any moisture before he slid back in under the duvet. Jane hadn't even noticed his absence, her sleep was so deep and untroubled. It took at least half an hour for him to drift off to sleep again, worried he would dream about the tornado once more... or something much worse. Surely not the bats again, he hoped.

Steve woke again the next morning with sun streaming in through the long bedroom window, directly into his eyes. The cream net curtains not doing much to diffuse the bright sunlight. He groaned. The scotch of the previous night was doing its early morning thing as usual. He hadn't remembered much of the previous night other than him and Jane fumbling at each other on the sofa and ending up in her bed. Then the memory of the dream hit him. He groaned.

"Morning, Steve," said a sweet voice. "Feeling better?" Jane's head was on Steve's chest listening to his slow heartbeat.

"Sort of," Steve replied. "I had an awful dream during the night. Scary."

"Was I really that bad?" she chuckled.

"Of course not," Steve grinned. "In fact you weren't in it. Well, you were, but I couldn't find you. I was reliving yesterday, but I couldn't get off the roof of the keep. I was trapped up there and got swept away by the tornado. I woke up before I died. Or I think I died. Anyway it's over and I'm here now."

"Christ, that's an awful nightmare... not being here with me, that is," she said soothingly and started to stroke his chest. "Fancy some breakfast? My special scrambled eggs and some strong coffee should help you forget all about that bad dream."

"Sounds great," he said as he watched her get out of bed and cover her nakedness with a purple silk dressing gown. Steve smiled at himself. She really was perfect, he thought. "By the way, how are you feeling after yesterday?" he asked.

"Surprisingly good. Last night helped a lot. It was a bit sooner than I had planned but I think we both needed that."

He smiled and nodded.

Steve slowly dragged himself out of bed himself a few minutes later, still smiling. "Okay if I take a quick shower, Jane?" he called out from the hallway to Jane who was in the kitchen preparing their breakfast.

"Sure, no problem," she replied as the smell of fresh toast and coffee wafted from the nearby kitchen." There are fresh towels in the bathroom cupboard and I'm sure you won't mind that girly body wash and shampoo just this once. I'll have to get you some of your own, won't I?"

Well, that's a good sign, thought Steve as he nakedly padded his way along the pale blue carpeted hallway to the small bathroom. He showered a little faster than usual, wanting to get back to Jane but really wanting her to join him. He was standing there with the hot water cascading onto his foggy head like a snare drum. Jane's shower gel did smell nice but if he told Pete he'd used it he's get the piss taken out of him royally. He hoped Pete wouldn't notice the sweet jasmine fragrance when he got to the office later.

The scrambled eggs on wholemeal toast were indeed special. "These are great," he said. "They taste very different, sort of spicy... unusual."

"Ah, that's what makes them special, my dear. I add a bit of coriander powder in the mix while I'm whisking and then do them for three minutes in the microwave. Much easier and quicker than using a pan. It's amazing what you see on Youtube when you are idly browsing and a bit bored at work."

"I love them," he said, stuffing another forkful of the toast and fluffy egg into his mouth. He swallowed and said, "I'm starting to love a lot of things these days." Sneakily vague, he thought, and looked at Jane for a reaction.

"Me too," she replied and smiled.

After breakfast was eaten and Steve had insisted on doing the washing up, Jane reminded him that he was supposed to be meeting Pete in the office. He reluctantly agreed. "I *would* prefer you to stay though," she grinned and winked.

"The feeling is mutual, but we can't have Pete sulking, can we? Jackie would never forgive us. And he's probably at work already getting up to all sorts and looking at his watch every couple of minutes and the door every five or six. See you tonight?"

"Definitely," replied Jane. "I'll nip out later get pick up some things. Bloke stuff, although you do smell pretty, Steve," she laughed cheekily.

"Sod off!" Steve playfully acted hurt by her words. He kissed her and then left the flat, grinning. Happy for the first time in years.

Jane sat at the kitchen table with another milky cup of coffee and planned her day. She decided to cook for Steve later. If he stuck around after that then it was a very good sign. She sipped her hot drink and made a list. Top of it was 'Bloke smellies!'.

Steve arrived at the office just after ten. As expected, Pete was there fiddling with something under the desk his main PC was sitting on.

"Put that thing away!" Steve joked.

"You okay, mate?" Pete said, looking a little put out. "Thought you'd be here earlier."

"Just had a lovely breakfast... with Jane," replied Steve.

"Oh," said Pete, now grinning. "The way things are going we'll be related soon," he sniggered.

"Don't start, you knob. We have plenty of work to do today."

"Fine, I have more piss-taking to do afterwards," laughed Pete.

"Does your wife know how much of a twat you are?" scowled Steve.

"Pretty much," grinned Pete. "So, seriously, how are you feeling after yesterday?"

"I'm fine, mate. Bloody relieved I was inside the tower and not one of those poor bastards outside. It must have been horrendous," he said.

"Yeah, I saw a bit of coverage on the news couldn't stand much of it to be honest, knowing you and Jane were there. Those poor sods never stood a chance. Either flung out to sea or smashed against the castle walls. They said it could take months for everyone to be identified, if that is even possible. I'd hate to be one of those poor buggers who had to collect all those body parts. I thought doing IT in a call centre was a shit job. Some of those who ended up in the channel may never be recovered. More chance of finding Glenn Miller out there, I'll bet."

"I did have a bitch of a dream last night though where I got caught in it."

"Shit, I'm not surprised though, it must have been terrifying for you both. Is Jane okay or still traumatised by yesterday?"

"She's good. It seems she recovered from it a lot better and quicker than me. I'm just glad we both survived, to be honest. Now that I've found Jane I really don't want to lose her," smiled Steve sheepishly.

"Jesus, you've got it bad," grinned Pete. "I've never seen you this hooked before."

"Well, you know, mate. Sometimes things just happen and this could make up for all the bad times in the past. You know what Stacey was like. I'd hate to still be married to her. Just imagine that!"

"Luckily Jane is nothing like Stacey. I only met your ex the once and that once was definitely enough for me, mate. I remember I called her 'The Wicked Bitch of the West'," Pete laughed.

"Don't remind me! I had heard Welsh girls were all lovely. It's all lies, you know, at least in her case, anyway."

"She did have a very nice chest though," said Pete.

"Aye, there was that!" laughed Steve. "Anyway, enough of that stroll down bad memory lane, let's get the broadcast planned for later on. You know I hate to script things too much but I need to get all of yesterday's events down on paper before it all goes out of my mind, while it's still fairly fresh."

"Okay. You get it all down with the help of a coffee and I'll get fiddling again," said Pete.

"You'll go blind, you know," laughed Steve, adding a wink for effect.

"Three sugars, dickhead," replied Pete.

Steve sat behind his desk staring blankly at the camera in front of him.

"You okay, Steve?" asked Pete.

"Yeah, this is going to be a hard one to do," frowned Steve.

"Just relax mate, it will all start to flow when you get started, just let me know when you are ready."

After a long minute, Steve said, "Okay, 3-2-1."

Pete started the camera recording and pointed at Steve.

"Afternoon everyone. Did you notice I didn't say good afternoon, people? As you already know there was another devastating disaster yesterday at Dover Castle, in Kent. You can't really have missed it. It's been all over the TV news and radio and every news website in the world. Well, believe it or not, I was there. Just as I was when those giant hailstones hit the BBC studio when I was doing that woke panel show with Mark Mason, the author. I don't know if its coincidence or bad luck or this Mother Earth, if that is what's responsible for all this, has it in for me for some bloody reason. I'd better watch my step from now on, I think, although none of us know when and where the next event will hit. Mother Earth - I know you are probably watching so please think about what you are doing. A lot of innocent people have died because of your actions. People who, I'm sure, do their very best to be sustainable. How do you feel about killing the very people who are trying to behave responsibly? Eating less meat, recycling and even up cycling things like furniture for God's sake? Does that make any sense to you? It doesn't to me and millions of others. These good people are not your enemy, are they? Those who are in power are. The manufacturing industry. The oil and coal industries. Just where will your 'judgment' end? Don't you ever feel guilty about what you are doing, Mother Earth? I know I would if I were the one doing all this. And why me? I've been caught up in your alleged attacks twice now. What the hell have I ever done to you? I recycle. I flatten my cardboard boxes and walk to the disgustingly smelly communal bins to get them picked up by equally smelly bin men. Sorry, any bin men, but you are! I even put my food waste in the appropriate container too. I don't drive much, I rarely fly either. I use public transport when I can. I'm pretty bloody innocent when it comes to the things that have upset you. I'm sure now that it's not a coincidence. You've told me that you are using me to get YOUR message

out there but you've nearly killed me twice. Are you bloody mental or what? It seems you are. What you are doing makes no sense. If you kill me then I won't be able to broadcast your ridiculous demands, will I, you idiot? You are murdering people and actually CAUSING more pollution in some cases - look at that dam in Pakistan, for example. The earthquake in Australia, what happened in Paris. Think of what it will take to clean up that lot! Thousands of Lorries, earth removal machines, meat wagons and ambulances - all chucking out even more emissions and making things a lot WORSE. Have you even thought about that, Mother Earth? Mass graves needed where trees could have been planted. Even if they use electric vehicles they are STILL charged by burning fossil fuels. What the hell is wrong with you? Have you been so brainwashed about the negatives of climate change that you don't even think about the difficulties implementing any of the solutions? It's not as easy as turning off a bloody light switch, is it? Just THINK about it for a second. Admittedly we produce more waste now than ever, but what is the solution? You can't burn it, you can't stick it in a landfill and you certainly can't bung it all in the bloody sea, can you? Should we send it all into space? So instead of using your immense 'power' by killing innocent people, why not use that power to solve these problems? Doesn't that make more sense? Anyway good people. I know that rant was not directed at any of you, because I know most of you are like me and try to do their bit for the planet. It was only at the person or thing responsible for all this crap. But maybe if we all think of better solutions to end pollution instead of making a bigger mess of this world then I can only think of that as a positive. I'm sure you regular viewers all know by now I'm not some sort of mental eco warrior. I won't block roads or chain myself to trees or any of that stuff because all that does is antagonise everyone and make you look like a Lefty idiot. So, good people, as I'm still a bit shaken about being in Dover yesterday, I won't be taking calls today but will read and respond to all your lovely comments. Take care everyone. Talk soon."

"That was great, Steve. Just what we wanted to goad Mother Earth into a response. Now all we have to do is monitor the comments after I upload the video - give me ten minutes and then hopefully Jane can do her stuff and for that MI5 tracking shit to work too," said Pete.

"Bugger. I've just thought about something else. Remember back in the day when everyone drove around using leaded petrol and all the factories were chucking out thick black smoke and before we had smokeless coal? There seemed to be a lot less pollution in this country than we have now. Maybe there is more to all this than meets the eye?" said Steve.

"Good point. Bottom line is that unless China and India start giving a toss and stop polluting then whatever the rest of us do is pretty pointless, mate," replied Pete. "Britain is doing a lot more than most countries, judging by all the taxes we pay. Look what drivers have had squeezed from them so far? Road tax, Insurance with an extra tax on top, fuel duty and VAT on whatever they pay at the pump, parking fees and permits, not to mention that congestion charge and having to buy ULEZ compliant cars or you have to cough up even more cash if you drive into London and a few other places. I don't think drivers in any other country in the world are screwed as much as us Brits. Just where does all that cash go? It certainly doesn't go towards a permanent solution to our knackered roads - potholes everywhere outside the cities. They fill them up and a couple of months later they are worse than ever."

"Totally agree mate. That's a great idea for a future show - how much British drivers are being ripped off, especially by the government and our lovely dwarf Mayor too."

Jane sat next to Pete and smiled nervously at Steve. She had been in the supermarket when Pete had called to ask her to come to the office to try and trace Mother Earth after the recording. Her appearance had been planned for the weekend but after yesterday the broadcast to trap Mother Earth was quickly brought forward. Jane didn't mind though. It meant she saw Steve before this evening and they could travel back to her place together when they were all done there. The sooner it was all finished, the sooner they could get back and have a nice romantic meal. They could stop off for a good bottle of wine on the way, as it has slipped her mind after Pete called.

While Pete did his tech magic and uploaded the video to Youtube, Steve and Jane sat on the leather sofa and drank coffee and chatted. Jane didn't seem to be too affected anymore about what had happened the previous day. She had been terrified at the time, of course, as was Steve, but it didn't take her long to recover her calm exterior. She was certainly made of stern stuff, he thought.

"We've gone live, Steve," said Pete. Steve and Jane rushed over to the main PC to check for comments. It was amazing how quickly some appeared. Steve supposed that was the point of notifications. As the views increased it only took a couple of minutes for the first comment to appear.

Georgina1981: "Hope you're OK, Steve, it must have been awful. I saw it on the news."

"Come on, Mother Earth," Pete whispered. "Come on you bitch!"

JesusLives: "You certainly had The Lord watching over you, Steve. Never forget that, man."

Lynne@The Bell Basingstoke: "Well said Steve. Anytime you are in the area drop in for a drink. Sounds like you need one, sweetie."

AmosBrearley2: "You gave that Mother Earth fecker what for, mate! Good on yer, son."

PriscillaPink: "You made an excellent point about this person or whatever making things a lot worse with these antics, Steve. It doesn't make a lot of sense to me either."

JohnnyBlade77: You gave that bloody Mayor what he deserves Steve. How does he get re-elected all the time with all the damage he's doing to Londoners? I have to turn down plumbing jobs in the capital because of my old diesel van. The alternative is stinging the customers for the charges which would be wrong but I know others in the trade are doing it."

MotherEarth: "What the hell do you think you are doing, Mr. Hansen? You know how much power I have and how I can use it. You say that you think I have targeted you? Well you are right. And that also means that I know where you are ALL THE TIME! It is certainly not wise to upset me like your father did! He paid the price and so will you eventually. Anytime I choose, sunshine. Remember that! I knew you could have escaped yesterday, so I kindly let you live. The other time too, because you were still useful to me. But after this frenzied attack on me today my patience has worn very thin with you, Mr. Hansen. I could very easily use others like I have used you. I chose you because of our past connection. Your father rejected me over forty years ago. Just because I didn't readily give into him, he dumped me and went off with your mother. But I made sure he suffered before he died in that car fire. It was just a small blaze at first but I made certain that he couldn't undo his seat belt or the doors and so he was trapped in that disgusting car. He screamed and thrashed about as the flames increased all around him but it was no use. Even though I was a couple of hundred yards away I could see him, see his contorted face, just as I can see you now. I see the girl you were with yesterday is there again. Will you use her like your father tried to use me? Maybe you won't get the chance. I have plans for you, Mr. Hansen. I guarantee you that. Just think. Had I known your mother was pregnant I would have finished her, and you, too. But at the time I just wanted her to suffer the heartbreak and the loss of your father like I did when he discarded me for her. I thought that punishment for taking him away from me was enough for her but I didn't take into account how much of a lecherous beast he was and had already impregnated her with you before he died so horribly. The sins of the father! I doubt you've ever read the Bible, have you, Mr. Hansen? The vengeful God of the First Testament is nothing compared to what I can do... and have done. He only managed a great flood, destroyed Sodom and Gomorrah, but I could end this planet with just a wave of my hand, or my mind, to be accurate. But that would be pointless, wouldn't it? It would defeat my purpose of saving this world we laughingly 'live' on. But if I need to I could destroy nearly all life on a global scale. Start all over again. People like you do sicken me, Mr. Hansen. You strut around thinking you are important but you, and everyone else, are nothing to me... and you mean nothing to this planet either. Ultimately just dust in the wind. So this is a final warning to you and everyone else. One month from today, unless the governments of the world prove to me they are making wholesale changes AND progress, I will destroy all humans on this earth, including myself... a Great Reset. Like I said, start all over again, and this time for the better. Maybe there will be people again in a few million years, but I do hope not. Let the flora and fauna rule this world! This message will also go out to every government and news channel on the planet. People will have to listen for once in their miserable unimportant lives. We shall not speak again, Mr. Hansen. Remember... ONE MONTH!"

"Jesus H. Christ!" said Pete. His hands were shaking. "What was that shit about your dad? Is she off her fucking rocker, mate?"

"I never knew my dad. He died before I was even born. My mum said he died in a car accident and she hadn't known him that long. That is pretty much all I know about him," replied an ashen Steve, visibly shaken.

"That's so bloody freaky. Worse than her saying she can actually see you... us!"

Steve looked towards the dingy polystyrene ceiling, smiled, and raised his middle finger at Mother Earth.

"That's the spirit, mate," said Pete through a nervous laugh.

They both then looked at Jane. She sat with her eyes closed with a map of Britain on her lap. Her right index finger lightly resting on the page and spiralling around the map, the circles were getting smaller, eventually fixing on one area.

"Any luck, Jane?" they asked in unison.

"Shhh!" she said softly, still with her eyes tightly shut. "If she is indeed watching us I don't want her to hear what I'm doing or saying."

After a few more minutes she looked at them and then down at the map, her finger now stationary. "Wiltshire!" she whispered, "South of Trowbrige, West of Salisbury. I'll need a better map, Pete."

Pete quickly found a detailed map on the internet of the area that was under Jane's finger. She stared at the screen. "Looks like the countryside around Bowerchalke, Barrow Hill, Woodminton Down. Pretty rural and out of the way," she said gently.

"Great job, Jane!" Steve smiled. "Proud of you, petal. It will be interesting if that MI5 spy software came up with the same area... if it worked at all," he whispered.

"I wonder if they'll even tell us," said Pete, quietly glum.

Hannover, Germany.
August 20th.

Tunde Kone had arrived in Germany just a few weeks previously. He had been scraping a living by begging outside hotels, before he was moved on, and at the nearby train station, where he had to compete with the other illegal immigrants. It had taken him several months to travel from the town of Sangha in the Democratic Republic of Congo to Hannover and needed to make enough money to continue his journey further west but it was taking him a long time as he wasn't making a lot of cash from the begging, barely enough to feed himself, although the odd kind person sometimes gave him a sandwich and a cup of coffee. He didn't feel too well at the moment and probably unable to travel anyway, he felt so tired. He'd seen many people like himself on his travels and thought there may be some king of sickness or bug going around. He hoped it would pass and he wouldn't need any treatment, as he couldn't afford to go to hospital. It was probably just one of those things that disappeared on its own with rest and plenty of water. He had been feeling very dehydrated and luckily he slept rough near the banks of the Leine river where he could drink plenty of water for free. It seemed a lot cleaner than the water in his own country. But whatever the amount he drank, he never felt fully sated by it. He thought it was because of the fairly cheap salty food he'd been eating and his body wasn't used to it. Weak, tired and thirsty - just a bug. He had no idea what he had brought into the country. Luckily for him he showed no real symptoms of the terrible disease as he was just a carrier.

Mady Schlachter lay on her bed in her small flat feeling awful. She was a prostitute who worked the hotels but never the streets. It was much safer and she had a better class of client than the losers who got their jollies in back alleys and in cars. Her clients were usually businessmen visiting Hannover, there for conferences, who stayed at mid-price hotels and fiddled their expenses enough to pay for Mady. Her body ached so much and her head throbbed as she rolled over and stared at the bowl of vomit on the floor beside her bed. She really needed to empty that as the smell was pretty disgusting. It looked like chicken soup but there were flecks of red which had floated to the top. She tried to move and get herself off the bed but she had no energy. She knew that if she didn't eat something soon she would never get any better, just a lot weaker. She had to make the effort because no one else would. She wasn't worried about not working. She could well afford a break and had several thousand Euros in the bank and even more in her savings account. A few days off would have done her a bit of good if she wasn't feeling so ill. She steeled herself, took a deep breath and swung her legs off the bed. Mady felt slightly dizzy as she staggered towards the bathroom and was relieved when she made it to the toilet bowl and sat down. She sat there for several minutes feeling faint. She wasn't sure if she could actually make it back to the bed let alone the planned excursion into the kitchen for some food and water. She tried to rise and then flopped down on the seat again feeling totally drained as her legs gave way. What the hell was wrong with her, she thought. She had caught various things from her clients before, those who had paid a lot extra for going bareback, but nothing this bad. She grabbed hold of the edge of the sink to her right and hauled herself to her feet. She was just about the flush the toilet when she noticed the bowl was full of red liquid. Then she started to panic. He had to get to the phone to call for an ambulance. Was she dying? Was there as much blood in there as she thought or had it been diluted by the water already in there? Either way she wasn't taking any chances. Mady shuffled towards the bathroom door. She could feel more blood dripping from her and running down her legs as she walked. She steadied herself by gripping the door frame and then she suddenly collapsed heavily in the hallway. The light green carpet rapidly becoming a deep red as her life drained from every orifice of her body. No one found Mady for several days. By that time hundreds were already afflicted with the outbreak.

Days later, Hansi Baumgarten was completely exhausted. He was an Emergency Room doctor at the Adler Klineken in central Hannover, and had been on duty for over fifty-six hours with only a few very short breaks. He found an empty examination room and lay on the bed and wearily closed his eyes. It seemed like the end of the world to him. Over four thousand patients and three thousand deaths so far in the last week just in Hannover. It had been confirmed as Ebola and it was spreading to other regions of the country rapidly. Berlin and Stuttgart were hit badly and it was reported to be heading for the Bavarian region where a few of his family still lived. He was extremely worried about them. He'd seen the odd isolated case of Ebola over the years but the patients were very quickly isolated and quarantined and were so sick the worst of their contagious period was behind them, so they rarely infected others by the time they were admitted to the hospital. He surmised that patient zero hadn't died for some time after coming into contact with the virus and had infected a lot of people and that had spread exponentially throughout first, Hannover and then half of Germany. They were a carrier - a Typhoid Mary, of sorts. He feared the disease may even spread worldwide. It was beginning to get totally out of control. The Robert Koch Institute, the German version of the CDC, had taken over and were trying to mastermind the fightback. Germany had begun to see the return of concentration camps and it would only be a matter of time before the government were forced to implement furnaces to dispose of the tens of thousands of bodies, maybe even millions. Something most Germans still felt shame about could well be a blessing this time and help control the spread of the infection. And possibly save what was left of the population. The army had been quickly brought in to remove the bodies of the dead from the hospitals and to respond to the frantic calls from the residents of the city when one of their loved ones showed any symptoms. The air force was used to ferry doctors from the Institute to various hospitals throughout the country. International aid was very quickly administered. Every country held a stock of Inmazeb, an experimental anti-Ebola drug, which would help arrest the rate of infection but it was still not a cure. Three quarters of those who had already contracted the disease would most likely die anyway, either from the massive blood loss or from a secondary infection. Millions of the ampules were airlifted to Germany from countries desperate not to suffer the same fate. It seemed there was some new crisis every week all around the world but they were mostly localised. Ebola could have a worldwide effect if it was not dealt with very quickly and efficiently. The whole world watched their news channels with growing fear. Years after the Berlin Wall was torn down, a virtual wall was erected all around the stricken country.

Marine Zulka was a nurse at the same Hannover hospital as Dr. Baumgarten. She had worked there for the past seven years since her youngest daughter had been born. Marine had been on duty on the night that the very first patient was brought in with what looked like some form of haemorrhagic fever. Although she quickly donned a face mask and gloves she had been infected within seconds without knowing it as the patient repeatedly coughed up blood and Marine bent over to console and reassure them that the staff would do everything possible to make them well again. Several other people were admitted that night, mostly of African origin but a couple of respectable looking businessmen too. At the end of a seemingly extra-long shift she then went home to the family she loved so much. A husband, Thomas, two daughters, Johanna and Ilse, and her elderly widowed mother, Lotte Wagner, who looked after the children during the day while Marine did her best to save lives and Thomas worked at the foundry on the other side of the city. The next morning the two girls were dropped off at school by their grandmother. Lotte then went on to the supermarket as she wanted to cook a special meal for her daughter who was very upset about the events of the previous day and worked so hard. At that time neither the girls nor the old woman felt anything was wrong with them. A week later the only survivor of the Zulka family was the husband. His wife, daughters and mother-in-law all gone by then. Their bodies has been taken away by the army to God knew where. Thomas Zulka had been kept in the dark by the authorities as to their fate. He'd heard rumours that all the dead bodies had been incinerated but he assumed something as terrible as that would be suppressed by the state media. He'd never know for sure what had happened to his loving family. He wept as he swallowed almost forty sleeping pills one by one. Why should he be the one spared? Why was he immune? Thomas was one of many indirect victim of the disease. He was found a week later when a work friend called in to find out why he had been absent from the foundry in the industrial area on the outskirts of the city where he had worked for nearly twenty years.

And that was how the virulent disease was spread very quickly. Mother to child, child to school friend, school friend to family. Workmate to workmate. The symptom-less incubation period lasted around two days on average... then it all escalated rapidly - the hospitals were swamped and looked like First World War battlegrounds. Hospital cleaners had barely mopped up one puddle of blood from the floors of the corridors when another was spotted a little further along, a never ending job, and of course the cleaners became infected too despite the protective gear they were wearing. It looked very hopeless to everyone, especially all the doctors and nurses on the front line of the battle to stop the epidemic. The German borders had been closed several days earlier, barbed wire strewn across roads and thousands of armed guards were deployed.

Dozens of desperate people had been shot while trying to escape but some had made it over the borders to Austria, Poland and France, sneaking through forests in the dead of night, torn and bloody from colliding with trees and bushes because they were too scared to use a flashlight to guide them, terrified of discovery. Some of them had already been infected but most had not.

Eventually the infection rate slowed down. They were making good progress and the Inmazeb had almost done its job. It was later officially upgraded from an experimental drug to the first line of defence against Ebola. It had been too late for Hansi Baumgarten, one of the first on the front line against the horrific disease. He had died in a concentration camp near Hamburg to the north of Hannover. At least his family members in Bavaria had luckily survived. The Ebola had been halted less than fifty miles from the region. Those lucky enough to have escaped the border guards were quickly rounded up in the surrounding countries and dealt with harshly. The world, already on high alert and fearful, had begun to breathe a sigh of relief at the news coming out from Germany. Most though, worried about the next disaster, and the next one after that. They were very certain they were not out of the woods as far as the many catastrophes worldwide were concerned.

Tunde Kone's badly emaciated body was eventually found in the bushes on the banks of the River Leine. No one knew he was the carrier as no post mortem was ever done on him. There were just too many other bodies found in houses, abandoned factories and in the fields near Hannover to autopsy them all. He was incinerated together with thousands of other dead. Most German people had lost someone they loved or someone they knew. It would take years to heal the people of that country.

GCHQ.
Gloucestershire, England.
August 30th.

John Thurston, one of the senior section chiefs at the spying and monitoring facility based in the English countryside, sat at his desk with the computer audit printouts in front of him. He sighed heavily. How the hell was he going to handle this? Vera Castle of all people! She'd been tracking someone called Steven Mark Hansen without any authorisation. Why? The logs had clearly shown what she had been doing. Was she working for a foreign government? If she was, then why him? Was he the spy? It didn't make sense either way. Hansen was just a Youtube celebrity, wasn't he? Thurston just didn't see the point. He'd personally checked out Hansen and there was no valid reason for him to be monitored at all. Hansen had even been to Downing Street to see the Prime Minister but that had been explained adequately by the Home Office. According to the report from them Hansen had been contacted by this person or group calling themselves Mother Earth and had been completely vetted and, other than being contacted by those claiming to cause the many fatalities, had no direct involvement with the disasters happening all around the world. The Prime Minister had summoned him but no official record of their conversation had been made, just a security report. So why was Vera Castle monitoring him? Was it something personal?

He was at a loss to explain it all. He was also unsure how to proceed. Would he just monitor her actions to try and get some sort of clue as to why she was doing this, or should he haul her in to his office and confront her? Either way he'd eventually need to discipline her. The resources at GCHQ were very valuable and the misuse of them was at least a sackable offence and had even led to a short prison stay in a few of cases in the past. He obviously didn't want her to be jailed. She was one of the best at her job. She wasn't liked much, but she was good at what she did and very experienced. She seemed to have some sort of sixth sense. How could she be so bloody stupid? She'd tried to hide what she'd been doing but the logs in front of him didn't lie. Even if she was a spy he just didn't see why this Hansen chap was so important to her or any foreign government she may be working for. If he asked for advice from a superior this could escalate very quickly and would probably even make the media. It could even mean his job too. He was only two years away from retirement so he couldn't afford to blow his whole career, not now. All those years wasted. All the sacrifices he'd made, including losing his family because of the long hours devoted to his career. He looked at the logs once more and sighed again. There was absolutely no doubt what she had been doing.

A red drop fell onto the reports. Then another. Thurston cursed the stress induced nose bleed and the reason behind it. He'd had them before over the years, especially after his acrimonious divorce. He reached into his waistcoat pocket and pulled out a pristine white handkerchief and held it gently to his nose. Thurston's head started to feel pressurised then started to throb and his vision blurred a little. This was more severe than the usual nose bleeds he'd suffered in the past. He pulled the handkerchief away and there was hardly any white left to see. He opened one of the desk draws to find his box of tissues and grabbed several and pressed them to his face. They soon became soaked too. Thurston pressed the intercom and asked his secretary to call for the site nurse to visit him. He was getting a little worried now as he was losing what seemed to be a lot of blood. He pulled more tissues from the box. His waste paper basket was starting to overflow with them. More and more tissues followed. They were strewn across the floor now.

Minutes later there as a tap at the door and the nurse entered. Jenny Moore was a petite redhead of around thirty-five. As soon as she saw him she rushed to his side. Thurston took the latest handful of tissues from his face and was about to say something when the blood gushed from his nose and mouth all over his desk. Every paper on it was soaked in the crimson fluid. Jenny pushed his head back to try and stop the flow but the blood was all over the front of him. Pints of it. Thurston was now very pale where he was not covered in blood and his lips had started to turn blue. Jenny pressed the blood stained intercom and shouted at the secretary to call for an ambulance urgently. Emergency! She had never seen anything like this before. Although she'd worked for the NHS for years before joining GCHQ, she'd never experienced anything remotely similar to this. It was like the blood was being squeezed from him somehow, like a sponge. She knew the ambulance would never arrive from the hospital several miles away in time and did her best to comfort him even though it looked hopeless. He needed a blood transfusion immediately and she didn't have the equipment to do it. Thurston looked into her eyes, he was now in total shock and as the remaining fluid gurgled in his throat he tried to tell her something. To her it sounded like 'very cassette'. It didn't make much sense to her. He coughed and sprayed her blue and white striped uniform with what little blood he had left. She thought his last words must have been his blood starved brain wandering aimlessly into oblivion, just a random thought. Thurston slowly closed his eyes and slumped heavily onto the desk.

Vera Castle heard the ambulance arrive as she sat at her desk, the two-tone siren blaring as it reached the car park at the front of the sprawling building. Her left hand was clenched as if she was wringing the water from a wet rag. She smiled slyly. She knew it was way too late for Thurston now. She was confident he was the only one who knew what she'd been up to, other than the techie who provided the reports to Thurston... and he would be dealt with later after all the commotion had died down. Probably a car crash on his way home later, before he could alert anyone else. She was safe to carry on with her agenda against the countries and governments causing the destruction of the world she had once loved, and that Steve Hansen, of course. She cared more about Nature than she did about anyone in her life and she wanted to exact revenge on those destroying it. Even her own life meant nothing to her anymore. Sacrifices had to be made - especially now that the deadline she gave the world governments was ticking away like a time bomb. Time was indeed ebbing away for her and more importantly, the planet and mankind.

Agnes Adebola, the office cleaner, was asked to try and make Thurston's office spotless after his medical emergency, and death, earlier that day. First she had walked around with a black plastic bin bag and, wearing latex gloves, she picked up the tissues from the floor, emptied the waste basket and moved on to the blood soaked papers from the desk into the bag, including all the evidence on Vera Castle. Then she used wash cloths and a sponge to soak up the large, congealing red mess on the desk and chair and squeezed it all into a bucket of water. She scrubbed the beige carpet but knew it would really have to be replaced. It was a stain she could never remove properly.

Mark Thompson, the techie who had found the unusual data and had presented it to Thurston, was driving home in his newly restored Triumph

TR6, looking forward to another marathon session on his game console. As he approached a busy roundabout the brakes on the old car failed and he ploughed into the back of a blue double decker school bus heading towards the centre of Gloucester. The TR6 burst into flames after the impact had killed Thompson almost immediately. A few seconds later the petrol tank exploded, sending a deadly conflagration in all directions, including the bus which was quickly enveloped in burning fuel. Thirty-seven children survived the accident and immolation - eleven, all seated at the back of the bus, didn't. When Vere Castle had heard about the collateral deaths connected to her murder of Mark Thompson, she was indifferent. Casualties of war, she thought.

Murton, North-East England.
September 1st.

Dawn rose slowly over the very small town of Murton, near Sunderland, in the North-East of England. It was very quiet with just the odd single car moving steadily through the deserted high street. It was slightly misty but it looked likely to be a lovely sunny day later according to the weather forecast for the area. A black helicopter hovered silently high above the sleepy town, not noticed by those few residents already up, having their breakfast and getting ready for work. Seagulls squawked loudly and flew off, watching the men dressed in black clothes manoeuvre themselves through the empty streets and alleys of the former pit town. The MI5 spy software had eventually given the location of Murton, and specifically, Coronation Street South and the operation had been meticulously planned. It was a quiet little road inhabited by mostly elderly people in old ex-pit houses. Coal production had ended in the town in the seventies and it had been almost a ghost town for years until a business park was set up on the outskirts of Murton in the early 2000s which did, at least, provide jobs for the younger people who had, until then, been leaving the town in their droves and moving out to Sunderland and Newcastle to find decent work. There had been some desperate times (and desperate people) in the area as each pit was systematically closed down one by one. Now very few mines remained anywhere in the North-East.

The small house in Coronation Street South was surrounded by the armed men. All was quiet and dark in the two up, two down, close to the end of the street. They had had the word from Command HQ. The front and back doors were simultaneously kicked in and a dozen men with assault rifles rushed quickly into the small house. Six of them ran up the stairs while the rest secured the downstairs area. They heard a frightened whimper from behind one of the doors leading off the landing. That door was also kicked down and a frail old woman in her eighties was sitting on a bed in a light blue night dress, frantically trying to get her white fluffy slippers onto her bony feet. She was visibly shaking with fear so much it was almost impossible, especially as two men had their rifles pointed at her torso, red dots wavered almost in unison, dancing across her skeletal chest. They shouted loudly at her to stay where she was and to show them her hands. She instantly complied and she looked like a bank robbery witness in an old western film, hands in the air and wondering if she would survive. One soldier held her at gunpoint while the other checked the room for anyone else and then went behind her and used green plastic ties to bind her liver spotted hands in the small of her back. She burst into tears as she was roughly bundled out of the house and into a black van that had pulled up outside in the street. All Lilly could think about was what was happening to her and what the neighbours would think of her. People she'd known most of her long life. The black van hurriedly drove away towards Newcastle.

Inside, the place was searched thoroughly, but they came up with absolutely nothing damning against the old woman except a tin of out-of-date fudge.

The squad leader exited through the back door into the small, unkempt garden, lit a cigarette, exhaled heavily and tapped the ear piece in his right ear.

"C7 reporting, Sir. Err, well, nothing to report really. We've been through this place from top to bottom and found nothing. No computer, or a tablet or any mobile phone for that matter. No devices at all. She doesn't even have an electric kettle!"

The reply from Command was an angry one. C7, (real name Sergeant Tom Watkins) was ordered to secure the house until the forensic people got there on the off chance they could yet find something the team had missed, but it looked like the information they'd received was false and the old woman had done nothing at all wrong. Watkins was told that she'd still be questioned but it seemed this frail old biddy wasn't Mother Earth after all. The spy software had given false information. This was embarrassing for everyone concerned. Especially those at MI5.

Lilly had been strip searched by a very butch female officer and given a matching grey sweatshirt and jogging bottoms to change into and also a pair of dirty sandals which were too big for her bony feet. She had been questioned relentlessly for several hours but it was fairly obvious she wasn't responsible for the disasters that had been happening all over the world. Not even as part of a group. She had never even heard of Youtube and had never even used the internet in her life. No modern equipment was found in her small house, even her TV was over twenty years old. The information they had got from MI5 was erroneous. Maybe even tampered with to give a false address.

The government and security services tried to keep the incident very quiet and out of the media but there was a leak from someone, probably at the police station in Newcastle. Two days later the full story came out - all the papers and news websites ran with the same facts - an elderly woman brutally arrested and subjected to 'torture' by authorities in the vain search for Mother Earth. Several top brass quickly resigned in the embarrassing aftermath. Lilly became the poster child (sort of) for the incompetence of government security agencies like MI5 and MI6 and there was a campaign started to get her massive compensation for the treatment of her by everyone involved in the fruitless raid.

London.
September 4th.

Steve sat at Jane's kitchen table reading a national newspaper in between bites of Jane's excellent scrambled eggs, now with coriander *and* cayenne pepper. They were a bit of a funny colour but Steve thought they were excellent - especially as the cayenne had been his idea to enhance the recipe.

"What a complete balls up," he said after sipping his black coffee. "So that software they installed came up with a totally different location to the one you found, it was only about five hundred miles off," he laughed.

"Poor woman," said Jane. "I can only imagine the panic she had to go through, considering her age she's lucky to have survived the shock."

"This compensation campaign will make her very comfortable for the rest of her life, I'm not sure she'd benefit from it for too long. That would have taken years off my life. I hope she has a few more years left in her but I suppose the grandkids will be very happy eventually. It's going to be millions with the compensation and the collection the public had donated to. Even I gave a fiver."

"So did I. Imagine them kicking my door down and bursting into the bedroom. Who knows what they'd see," Jane laughed and winked.

Steve almost blushed.

"I'll need to get hold of someone to tell them that our own star psychic came up with a different location. It's going to be more difficult since that dick Garland has been kicked out. Who ya gonna call?"

"I won't say it," grinned Jane.

Vera Castle sat reading her newspaper and laughed heartily. She'd known what was going on. She'd seen the security techs installing the spy software and knew Steve Hansen was deliberately goading her to respond so they could trace her. But she had been very clever and used her telekinetic ability to reroute her message back to him from another part of the country. They must have thought she was very stupid. She did feel a little regret for what that old woman had gone through. It would have been better if the house was shared by two or three young lads with a few computers and phones just to make it harder for them to dismiss that address so quickly, even after the search. Maybe even some conspiracy theorist who was on social media all day. It probably would have given her a lot more time. Still, it showed them all up to be idiots, didn't it? The public had lost faith in their own security services. Even though she was part of that same branch she felt a lot of pride in her clever deception.

Los Angeles, California.
September 7th.

The bright warm sun shone high in the Californian sky. It was a fairly normal day in Hollywood. Lots of activity around the various film studios, small and large. Tony Hale looked up at the sky, his green eyes shielded by his expensive sunglasses. He was one of the most famous actors on the planet and like quite a few of the Hollywood elite he had a deep, dark secret which he was desperate to keep out of the public domain. Rumours had been rife for years about his alleged ritual child abuse and visits to an island run by a multi-millionaire for celebrities and politicians to use and abuse small children, even allegedly murder them in extreme cases. Everyone who visited the island, including former Presidents, were protected by clever lawyers with even more clever super injunctions. Everything was hushed up by the people with power, influence and money... especially money. Tony Hale knew that once the money had begun to run out, that was when the vague rumours became full blown accusations against him and others. Luckily for him he'd made over a dozen box office smash hits so the royalties kept rolling in and would do so well into his old age. He was also protected by his wife. A third-rate actress who kept getting work as a reward for her silence about his activities. She knew she only had two real options. Either keep quiet and keep working and enjoy the lifestyle of being married to one of the world's most popular and richest actors... or mysteriously disappear after a boating accident or a plane crash in a remote region. So far, she was not a complication he'd had to deal with. He wondered if that would change if his popularity waned.

Tony appeared on the sound stage to start filming for the day. A new, although a well-worn genre, Romantic Comedy called 'I Had to Leave a Voicemail'. After a quick word with the director, Adam Fletcher, a man more known for directing the odd episode of long running TV shows and soaps and was now being given a chance at a big film after recently becoming a part of the same exclusive 'club' as Tony Hale. Adam had just returned from the private island himself and, given the amount of things he knew about other people now, knew he was in the big time for good. They knew things about him too now so the ring of silence spun in both directions. They used to say it was *who* you knew in Hollywood that made you successful, but that changed to *what* you know a few decades ago. Adam Fletcher was now one of the beneficiaries.

Melissa Mayberry, the skinny co-star, flaunted herself onto the set. As usual, Tony Hale's love interest in the film was almost thirty years younger than him, something his fans never seemed to think strange. After fake hugs and a few even more fake compliments they took their places in front of the camera. It took seventeen takes to get the first scene right. Either Tony or the director wasn't happy with Melissa. The actress kept wandering off from her mark on the studio floor and getting out of shot or kept fluffing her very simple lines. What was so hard about saying 'I flew far to fly back to you and now we can fly away together' or 'Why did you text me when I was standing right next to you?' Tony thought she should have been more professional and known the lines backwards as well as forwards and inside out like he did. He'd realised over the years that it was very rare for an actress to be pretty and actually be a good at her job too. But the stupid audiences lapped it all up. Totally brain dead idiots who cared more about which kind of coffee and sprinkles they wanted to have that morning than anything else. And L.A. was a prime example of these vacuous people, where looks and impressions meant everything. They all wanted to be noticed and become reality TV stars - already veterans of plastic surgery by the time they had reached their late teens. Truth be told, he hated these people but their money made him very rich so he hid his contempt behind his 'nice guy' public persona and a lop-sided smile. If only they knew the real him and about his trips to that island. He thought these stupidly vain people would be perfectly happy to be run over by a truck on Rodeo Drive as long as their corpse looked good for their friends to post on social media.

Over the years people had found out small things about him. Totally by accident. Then they had to be either paid off or they had a mysterious mishap that always ended in tragedy. He had far too much to lose when it came to the threat of being blackmailed. Even the fact that someone was blackmailing him would get out too and would rouse more suspicion, possibly even an investigation into his secret life. The film industry had always had its handlers, mysterious people lurking in the shadows, ready to deal with any problem they were told to by the studio bosses, producers and stars. Any time someone dies in Hollywood you can usually be sure the 'accident' wasn't really an accident at all. It was just a blessing for the others who were being protected. People who were close to exposing the wrongdoings of others in the business, but had told the wrong person of their intentions. Plain and simple, they were murdered to keep them quiet. Shot in a staged coffee shop 'robbery', brakes failing on the winding roads of the California hills, drowning mysteriously during the night while their husband was sound asleep on their boat. Even found floating in their hot tub at home with drugs planted nearby. Everyone in the movie business knew which deaths were not natural, but very few knew exactly why. Some had their suspicions but were wise enough to keep them to themselves, even from their closest friends because at the end of the day those friends could very well be competing for the same parts... and Hollywood was a dog eat dog world where friendships are mostly fake and actors would do literally anything for fame and fortune and their chance to become one of the elite like Tony Hale. Many actors in the past had been stabbed in the back (some even literally) for a role.

After an excruciatingly long two hours, due to the useless co-star, there was a break in filming while the set was changed for the next set of scenes and the director reviewed the footage. Tony was relaxing on a fairly uncomfortable canvas and steel chair in front of the trailer he was using when he wasn't needed on set. His agent, Maury Finkelstein, was seated next to him, briefing Tony on various possible future projects. Tony told Maury that he wanted to start directing, calling the shots for himself. Or maybe a drama that would get him another Oscar. Critical acclaim for his work. No more Rom Coms! He knew his fans were getting a bit bored with him doing mostly the same things. His legacy was still not complete... and more money was to be made for everyone which was key to his survival in the business. He knew he would be protected as long as he was very successful. His secrets were safe if he made even more money for those who had kept them. Maury Finkelstein was one of those people.

The giant object got closer by the second. Soon it would easily block out the warm Californian sun. Approaching silently and unnoticed... and very deadly. NORAD detected it far too late to warn anyone or use missiles to either try to destroy or deflect it. The asteroid was too close now and would definitely hit somewhere around the coast of Western California. The minutes passed. An emergency call to the President and the Joint Chiefs was received but there was no action other than to plan a press conference to try to deal with the aftermath. Afterwards questions would be asked, but there was no time for that just yet. America, and President Darnell Best, were totally unprepared for this. Anywhere else in the world would be unprepared for such a disaster too. People would know that films like Armageddon and Deep Impact, although entertaining, were fictional and nothing could really be done to avert an asteroid or meteor strike. Not even Bruce Willis could save them.

Tony looked up as the sky darkened rapidly. He removed his sunglasses for a better look. At first he couldn't make out what it was in the sky. Then the relatively tiny rocks which preceded the big one started to fall. Maury was one of the very first victims. A space rock the size of his fist slammed straight into his head, totally obliterating it. Tony quickly realised what was happening, rose swiftly from his chair and left it sprawled on its side next to the door of the large trailer. He started to run. He'd never run so fast in his whole life, not even in his most famous film. He had to quickly find some shelter. But where? He knew this studio lot like the back of his hand but panic was starting to grip him in its icy fist. Everyone on the set were now screaming and running in different directions as the small projectiles rained down on them. Some were struck mid-stride and their bodies ended up as unrecognisable heaps on the ground. Some people fell and were crushed by other people rather than the inevitable asteroid heading their way. The narrow roads between the sound stages were splattered with blood as the relentless attack from above continued. Tony then saw his chance. A row of large metal dumpsters sat alongside the building used as the main canteen. He sprinted towards them, throwing and pushing people out of his way. He had to survive, maybe even direct a film about his experience, he thought strangely. Tony reached the dumpsters and flung open the lid of the nearest one. The stench, made worse by the stifling Californian heat, was incredible. Tony gagged but still climbed inside and quickly closed the lid and sat in the darkness, shivering with fear in the cloying stink. What the hell was happening? Maury was dead and gone. He'd never seen anything like it. Not even a special effect in a film could be that gruesome as the death of his long time agent and friend. As he sat there, covered in grime and food waste, he could hear the screams and explosions of the relentless attack. No sound was muffled inside his haven. Rocks bounced heavily off the dumpster. He was going to make it. He was safe, he thought, and smiled grimly. Someone had tried to follow him into the dumpster but he used all his strength to prevent the lid from being opened, then he heard a blood-curdling scream. He wondered how long this onslaught would last, how long it would be until he could emerge from this sanctuary and back into the real world, safe. He couldn't wait until he was interviewed about his horrifying experience. More publicity, he thought. He'd be a hero for just surviving the disaster.

The asteroid was only small, in asteroid terms, that is. Just the size of a cruise ship. But the force generated as it hit Los Angeles threw millions of tons of debris into the air, including a certain dumpster on a studio lot. Tony was quite fortunate as the asteroid hit the ground. The shock wave flung his head violently against the side of the heavy container and he mercifully lost consciousness. Tony Hale died where he ultimately belonged in life. Just human trash in a metal container full of rotting food, plastic and rat shit.

The total area of devastation spread for mile upon mile. The death toll would never be known, of course. Even an estimate would be almost impossible. Residents, tourists, shoppers - all gone now. Many were just instantly vaporised by the massive asteroid impact. A state of emergency was declared by the tearful President, Darnell Best. The damage and loss of life would far exceed the disaster at Yellowstone Park. The world mourned. Not too many mourned for Tony Hale in the coming weeks as details of his secret life emerged. He wasn't making money for anyone anymore, so what was the point of protecting him? Half of Hollywood's elite were now looking over their shoulders. The West coast film industry had been devastated and they all worried about making enough money to remain protected. Hollywood provided around forty percent of the jobs in the movie business although a lot of the lower budget films were made in Romania and Hungary to save money. Hundreds were made in Canada too, Toronto doubling for L.A. or New York. Billions in investments had been wiped out within minutes. Anything recovered from the insurance policies would take months or even years to pay off. Those lucky enough to be working on location that fateful day never mourned their friends and colleagues. They just worried about being found out eventually. Especially anyone connected to Tony Hale.

Obviously, this was world-wide news. Not only because of the devastating loss of life and property but it plunged a massive part of the entertainment industry into turmoil it may not recover from. Dozens of shows were cancelled because most of their stars were either dead or missing. Sponsors pulled the plug on their deals because, as the shows were not on TV, there was no point in sponsoring them, so they turned to other areas to advertise, mainly sports. Film and TV fans were desolate as their favourite actors died horribly when the asteroid hit Hollywood that day.

Back in rural Wiltshire, England, Mother Earth sat in front of the TV in her favourite, worn cloth armchair. Between sips of tea she smiled smugly to herself. This was maybe the best one yet. The victims were not anonymous to the rest of the world so it would have a far greater impact. She laughed at the pun. It was a bigger, more potent, message to the people. Just let Steve Hansen comment on this on his poxy little podcast about the asteroid. She certainly showed him, and the rest of the world, her power over everything - even in the outer reaches of space. Her power was growing - far from the time when she had to be in fairly close proximity to the things and people she had an effect on. She'd come a long way over the years but this event had taken its toll and she had to rest for a few days. She suddenly thought she'd been very stupid. Why did she tell Steve Hansen about her connection to his father? Fool! It was so careless, her rage at him had got the better of her and she realised that was his intention. She wondered if it would make her easier to trace. Maybe someone from university had remembered her romance with Gerald and knew Steve Hansen was his son? Vera knew the tracking software had failed to reveal her whereabouts, but she needed to carry on her crusade on behalf of the planet and was desperate not to be stopped at this late stage. She had plans for other potential disasters. A localised ice age in Russia, a gigantic fire in the rain forests of Brazil, the Hawaiian islands sinking beneath the ocean, just like Atlantis was supposed to have done thousands of years ago. Fires, floods, plane crashes, ships sinking and plagues all over the world. No, no one could stop her. If they did manage to catch her she could still do all that from a prison cell for as long as she lived. They would have to release her before she *really* went to extremes. They had seen very little of her vengeance so far in her opinion. Time was still running out for her though. She tried to ignore the inevitable.

She thought about Gerald again. She remembered watching him from a park opposite where he lived with that whore he was shacked up with. Gerald Muffett was not a very nice man. She wondered if Steve actually knew that was his father's name. Muffett! Such a stupid name for a stupid, ignorant person. He certainly muffed it with her! He wasn't intelligent enough to realise that all those little mishaps he'd suffered over the previous months were all caused by her. He probably thought nothing of what was happening to him - maybe put it down to bad luck or his own stupid clumsiness. From someone running over his foot in a car park to tripping and falling down an escalator at a tube station, it was all down to her. Vera eventually got bored with these minor mishaps she was causing him and decided to finish him off for good. It was what he ultimately deserved after the way he had treated her.

He'd probably forgotten all about her by now. People like him move on very quickly to other people, another victim in her eyes, and they forget about their past and their bad deeds, oblivious to the way they had hurt people. He had no conscience, none at all. He would be called a sociopath now. Anyway, she certainly didn't forget about him. She wanted to make his life a living hell. The little accidents she willed upon him were not enough for her anymore. Gerald really had to pay for what he had done to her. He didn't see her in the unlit park across the road as he strode confidently towards his car, a battered old Ford Cortina with more rust patches than the original light blue paintwork. The door creaked loudly as he pulled it open then he sat in the tatty plastic driver's seat. She remembered how nasty and sticky the seats in that car were when he took her for a day trip down to Hastings. She hated peeling herself off the dirty plastic when they'd arrived there after a two hour drive. They pottered around on that dreadful stony beach before buying some fish and chips wrapped in old newspaper and then driving home when it started to rain heavily. What an awful day it was for her. He'd tried it on with her again, of course. Filthy pig!

Gerald took the car keys, attached to a small pair of furry dice, out of his worn, brown checked jacket and slid the ignition key into its slot on the grimy dashboard. The starter motor ground and squealed for a few seconds, draining the battery slightly, before the old engine caught. Gerald fitted his seat belt around him, put the car into gear and prepared to pull away from the kerb. He didn't know that the fuel line had been leaking onto the engine, caused by Vera, of course. Flames shot from the engine compartment as the fuel ignited, the paintwork of the bonnet started to bubble. Gerald quickly turned off the engine and tried to unclasp the seat belt. It was stuck fast. He frantically pulled at it, but it didn't budge at all. He then started to shout for help but it was past ten-thirty in the evening and there was no one hanging around the block of flats where he was living with Sandra Hansen. The handle for the driver's side window broke off. He banged heavily on the windows with his fists hoping to break the glass and have something to cut the strap of the seat belt with but all he managed was to badly bruise himself. Gerald tried to punch through the glass with his elbow but even that failed too. He urged his trapped body to stretch to the other side of the car and he just managed to reach the glove compartment with his left hand and it flopped open. He searched in vain for anything useful. In there was just an unopened packet of condoms and half a pack of Wrigley's chewing gum. Everything that was useful was in his tool bag locked safely away in the boot. He'd give anything for the Stanley knife floating around inside that bag, even a pair of pliers would do. He was screaming now as the fumes of the melting dashboard hit him. He started to cough and choke on thick black smoke and was now very close to unconsciousness. Gerald then saw the flames lapping at him from under the foot well and felt the searing pain as his worn polyester trousers caught fire. The conflagration spumed from the air vents like a miniature flame thrower. The sleeve of his jacket caught fire. More incredibly unbearable pain. The fire spread over the rest of his cheap clothes, the inside of the car full of the choking black smoke now. He tugged at the seat belt once again in vain. A passerby tried to open the car door but the heat of the door handle burnt him badly so all he could do was look on in horror when Gerald's burning head fell heavily against the window, cracking it slightly. From her position in the park Vera could hear sirens in the distance and she calmly walked away towards home, humming an 80s tune. Strangely she couldn't remember which one. Probably Culture Club or Duran Duran, she thought, something jolly and uplifting.

After emptying the tea pot at her side into a small china cup, she spent the next hour or so thinking of ways to dispose of *Mister* Steve Hansen. Fire like his useless father? No. Maybe he could choke to death, which would be slow and terrifying, asphyxiate on his girlfriend's cooking? That would be a belly laugh and almost poetic to her. She wondered if the girl was pregnant yet. This time she'd deal with her too, just in case, instead of letting Sandra Hansen live like she did all those years ago, bringing up Hansen to be the pathetic excuse for a human being he was.

Unknown to Vera Castle, Steve Hansen had contacted the Home Office to relay the real location of Mother Earth to the security services. At first they didn't believe him and dismissed the information he wanted to give but on the third desperate call they had started to listen. They knew any lead had to be checked out. They had been inundated with calls from people professing to have knowledge of the terrorist's whereabouts. Steve's persistence was a factor though. He eventually told them the precise area that Mother Earth was operating from. Images from a spy satellite showed a remote farmhouse and then a brief investigation told them that a Vera Castle lived there alone and she worked at GCHQ which had be the site of a few mysterious deaths very recently, was that down to her? Alex Porter, head of MI5 was fairly convinced and passed the Intel onto the Military Intelligence. He wanted her captured and interrogated... even tortured if need be. Did they finally have Mother Earth? He certainly hoped so. Then maybe the nightmare the world had endured over the last nine months would finally be over.

Hartlepool, England.
September 11th.

Hartlepool was famous for two things normally. A bad football team and the infamous monkey hanging incident when, during the Napoleonic Wars, a shipwrecked ape was believed to be a French spy and hanged by the locals of the North-Eastern town. The resident were forever to be known as 'monkey hangers' when it came to a bit of regional banter. What most people didn't realise was the other thing Hartlepool should have been famous for - a huge nuclear power station in the area.

Everything was perfectly run there as usual, the safety factor of these facilities had improved so much since the sixties, and even after Chernobyl, safety measures were tightened up even more. No one wanted a repeat of that particular disaster. If it happened to a British nuclear facility then not much of the country would even be habitable. The industry was the safest in the entire country though. It was monitored by the minute and also had several backup systems to detect any problem almost before it happened, and fail safes to deal with anything that could potentially cause a problem. They had never been needed. It was the same at every single nuclear facility around the world, even in countries like Iran. No one could afford an accident. Everything was checked and re-checked... and then checked again. Not even sabotage was a factor anymore. Or so they thought.

Vera Castle knew she had to make one last statement. Time had run out and she knew they were coming for her and would find her eventually. She needed to escalate things now, there was no other solution than a total reset of the earth. Those millions of deaths in France and Pakistan didn't manage to persuade the politicians, or at least convince them they had to act fast enough. None of the other disasters she had created had worked. It seemed every country, or at least their leaders, still doubted her ability to destroy the world. It was now time.

Vera had been to the Hartlepool power station in the past as part of a team to check the security of the place two years previously. Her role was to check the encryption of the computer system and its protection from the threat of a terrorist cyber-attack. She remembered roughly how the place was laid out, the reactors and the busy control rooms in particular. She concentrated on the site. She could remotely see the technicians working, constantly checking the vital safety systems. She started to control the workers. They were on a sort of auto-pilot now. Moving between various monitors displaying the lines and graphs and meters, viewing what they had seen countless times in the past and recording data on their half-hourly report sheets. With that out of the way Vera concentrated on the reactors. The core temperature started to increase very gradually. Normally this would have quickly triggered alarms all over the facility. The system would have begun to reduce power until the fault was found or a decision was made to shut down completely. There were no alarms though, and the technicians continued to see what they had always seen - clear boards everywhere. Things appeared safe to them.

Wiltshire, England.

Colin Wells of British Military Intelligence was getting his final briefing from Brigadier-General Alan Truscott in the mobile command centre, parked in a field less than three miles away from the farmhouse of Vera Castle on the outskirts of Bowerchalke. After the location tip-off from Steve Hansen, the military had investigated Vera Castle and concluded that the many 'coincidences' that had surrounded her over the years, culminating with the deaths of her boss at GCHQ and the techie who tried to expose her, was down to a strange, destructive ability from her mind. They now knew that ability to kill people remotely had been responsible for the many deaths all over the world over the last nine months. This was their last chance to stop her.

"You know the layout of the property, Wells," said the Brigadier. "Get in there as quickly and as quietly as you can and apprehend the woman. You know how dangerous she potentially is, so be very careful and if things start to go wrong then you know what to do. There is no Plan B, you understand?"

"Yes Sir," responded Wells curtly. "I realise how difficult the situation is and I'll do my best to take her alive."

Wells re-checked his equipment yet again and left the command centre. He would have to walk to the target in the pitch black. No one wanted him to alert the woman before he got there so any form of transport was not an option. The road he was on had been blocked off at both ends so there would be no traffic at all as he made his way to the remote farmhouse, shielded by a tall roadside hedge and the darkness of the still night.

The reactors at Hartlepool power station continued to slowly increase in temperature. Still no alarms or any indication from the system to indicate anything was wrong there. The staff were virtually sleepwalking around the place, totally unaware what was happening and the amount of time left to stop a massive explosion, destruction, loss of life and the end of Britain as a viable country was getting short. Now the same was happening in several other countries - hundreds of reactors were overloading while staff walked around as if nothing was happening. Vera Castle's power enveloped the whole world and it would end everything within a few minutes.

Wells silently approached the remote farm. There were no street lights in the secluded country lane which aided him. It was dark and easy for him to remain undetected, dressed in his black combat gear. He could see there was no light on downstairs but there was the slight flicker indicative of a TV being watched. Wells crept around to the back of the house and found the kitchen door was unlocked. He turned the door knob gently and silently and entered the rear. He could hear a British sitcom playing from the front of the house, but it was one he didn't recognise. Lots of fake laughter coming from the TV. A headache was now forming, some dark force was invading his brain. He knew Vera Castle was causing it. She must be sensing his presence in the house. He knew how powerful she was, causing all those disasters with just the dark force contained inside her mind. He needed to act fast or he would fail in his vital mission. He now knew for certain that he would not be able to capture her alive. He needed to take her out as soon as possible and avert any more death and destruction around the world. His assault rifle was held ready, finger resting alongside the trigger guard, poised to kill. There was no Plan B as Truscott had said earlier.

He padded slowly towards the front room, approaching the noise of the TV. He had to remain alert, had to anticipate where in the room she was. Sitting down? Waiting for him behind the door? She knew he was there. Was she just standing facing the door, waiting for him to act? Very unlikely, he thought.

Another sharp stabbing pain spiked in his head and almost brought him to his knees. Hot knives penetrated his brain from so many different angles. He had to fight through it. Not just for him but for everyone else on the planet. Was she causing permanent damage? Wells tried to put the thought out of his mind. Come on, Col, he desperately thought to himself. He took a last deep breath, held it, focused, and burst through the living room door, rolled to his left, and then came up into a crouching position, scanning the room. Where was she? The 70s sitcom on the TV was unwatched - now an obvious decoy. She must be hiding. Where though? The intense pain in his head was increasing by the second. It was almost unbearable and he knew he was close to passing out. He had to find her very quickly and stop her... permanently. He knew time was almost up for him.

Vera suddenly appeared. Looming large and filling the open door behind him. He looked into her puffy red face. She was smiling at him. Not a welcoming one though - evil. Her eyes were silver orbs, they looked alien to him. He was suddenly terrified of her.

"I saw you when you were hundreds of yards from the house. In my mind," she said coldly. "You are here to kill me, aren't you? Trying to stop me any way you can."

"N-No. Just to bring you in, we need to talk to you, study you, find out where your ability comes from, maybe use it for good! We need your help," he replied through the intense pain and fear.

"Do you think I'm that stupid?" she said. "I can read your mind! Your orders were to bring me in if you can and if not, I was to be eliminated. I already know you have dismissed the first option. You have no choice but to kill me now."

A sharp pain hit his right wrist, his hand snapping to the side, bones breaking easily. He had to release the deadly weapon and it flew across the room, propelled by an unseen force. Now red flecks appeared in her silver eyes swirling in a tight spiral. Wells was forced to the ground immersed in excruciating pain. His whole body then slid across the cheap beige carpet until he was sat up against the wall, slightly dazed. He could smell strong ozone in the air all around him. It filled the room.

"For years no one ever listened to me. I told them they were destroying the planet but greed always came first, didn't it?" she spat. "All this could have been avoided. They did not know about my abilities though. No one did. They all thought I was just a tiny, anonymous person working towards my inevitable retirement. How wrong they were, though!" she laughed loudly. Confident now the man was unarmed, and seemingly harmless.

"You murdered millions of innocent people!" screamed Wells, both in anger and pain. "Maybe even close to a billion worldwide, you bitch!"

"Innocent? Innocent?" she screamed. "Oh yes, they all did their bit recycling. Some bought electric cars or took their own bags to the supermarket! Bags for Life? Ha! But it was never enough. Companies made billions from the scams. Energy providers were the worst. Pretending to be green, getting a tiny proportion of their power from wind and solar while still relying of fossil fuels to make massive profits. Prices rising while the resources were depleting. Squeezing every penny they could from the consumers. Scum! All of them! Nothing but profiteers!"

"We could use your power to generate energy. Is that possible? Make those companies redundant. Can you do that?" asked Wells.

"Maybe at one time, if they had listened to alternatives. I can't now, though," she replied.

"Why not? Surely you have the ability to do some good for the planet?" he said.

"Because every time I've used my power to create these events over the world the tumour in my head has increased in size. My power has increased in intensity but the control of it has diminished. At one time I could have used it in short bursts with no ill effects to myself, just needing a short rest, but I've had to intensify my efforts recently to show the whole world the damage they were doing. I tried to scare them into action before it was too late!"

"So what is the answer now?" he asked.

"There is only one course of action, a total reset of planet earth. Start again. Maybe human life will evolve again, but it could take a hundred thousand years, maybe millions, who knows? I'd say it's best for the planet if it doesn't, considering the mess we made of it this time."

"A reset? How?" Wells asked.

"Total destruction... of everything. Back to the basic life this world started off with, bacteria. Evolve again from that point. It will take millions or even billions of years to get this planet back to what it deserves. Peace and tranquillity initially, then evolving into productive, innocent life without the same mistakes we made. Millions of years without the industrialisation which has virtually destroyed this planet. Just think of it!"

"How do you think that could possibly happen? There are nearly eight billion people on the planet. How do you plan to get rid of them?" he asked.

"I will use what is left of my power and explode every single nuclear power station in the world at the same time. Cause a total holocaust, catastrophe at its most potent. It's the *only* way. Imagine thousands of Chernobyls, all working together to create a better place?" she said calmly. Her silver eyes glinting, boring into the brain of Wells.

"You are totally mad, don't you realise that? The problems can be solved if everyone worked together. I think they will now that you have shown them they desperately need to act!" he said.

"No. They have all had their chance. They didn't care. Oh, they may show a little willingness at first but you know as well as I do that they will abandon their efforts again eventually. My way is better. It's the only way! After all, you were sent to stop me so that they can continue raping this planet for huge profit. They won't change. It's far too late."

She was so animated, so absorbed in her rant that she did not notice Wells' left hand moving towards his foot. His fingers snaked around the butt of the revolver in its ankle holster. Trying to put the massive pain in his head to one side he pulled the gun from the holster. Before Vera could react he fired once. A small red hole appeared in the centre of her forehead and she suddenly froze, a look of shock on her puffy face. He continued to fire into her head as she sunk to her knees. The remaining five bullets obliterating her brain. That grey and pink lump of immense power. Power that could have provided the energy to save the planet instead of trying to destroy it. The severe pain in his own head began to subside. He dropped the revolver and reached for his phone inside his loose black combat jacket. He reported to his superiors that the job was complete. Vera Castle was dead and wasn't a threat anymore and he requested a medic to come to deal with his broken wrist. Another mission successfully completed. But how successful in the long run? He thought. Then he passed out.

The nuclear reactors all over the world started to decrease in temperature and intensity. Alarms sounded at every facility and the technicians all snapped out of their trances and started to panic. Frantic orders were barked out in several languages around the globe. The security systems started to fire up. Wells had no idea yet, but the bullets he'd put into Vera's head had saved the whole world from total annihilation with mere seconds to spare. Her immense power was destroyed just in time. She had known she was going to die as soon as she sensed Wells was on his way to her farmhouse. She knew there was no way out for her so she'd decided that the whole of the wasteful, planet killing humankind had to suffer the same fate. It was the ultimate sacrifice in her eyes.

Earth had to survive after that reset. If she'd survived just a few seconds longer the whole world would have been gone - a total reset earth.

London.
September 17th.

Steve prepared to do his final Youtube broadcast for a while. He'd decided he needed a long break, to get away from it all for a while. A holiday somewhere sunny with Jane was definitely on the cards. Maybe a honeymoon? It was something to think about. The public had never known her part in saving the planet and that was how they liked it. No media attention. Nice and peaceful for them both.

"Good morning, good people. And it is a very good morning. Finally the truth can be revealed and the mystery is now solved. For a while I'd convinced you all that a supernatural entity, 'Mother Earth', was sending me emails warning us all about climate change and everything that goes with it. I was fooled too. But maybe the real explanation is just as frightening and just as mysterious. A woman, I'll avoid calling her mad, was behind it all. She was apparently a cryptographer and cyber specialist for the Ministry of Defence at GCHQ in Gloucestershire. That probably explains how she managed to send the emails from out of nowhere with no originating account or IP address and had a massive degree of encryption. So at least we know that's possible, and makes you wonder what other technical trickery the military and security services have up their sleeves, doesn't it? Anyway, this woman had an incredible mind but it turned out to be very warped and very angry. She had kept a diary and it turns out she had discovered her 'talent' for want of a better word, when she was quite young and the victim of bullying at school. Telekinesis is a proven fact and has allegedly secretly been used by the military for decades. The irony is the most gifted of them actually worked for the MoD for years and they had no idea of her real power, no inkling of her frightening ability. According to people in, and out, of the service she had been trying to convince everyone to save the planet for years. It mostly fell on deaf ears. Maybe she should have revealed her powers years ago? Maybe to do some good, try to generate her own energy that could have been used as an alternative to fossil fuels. Unfortunately, she kept quiet, only spilling out her thoughts in her diaries. In the subsequent decades, countries produced more and more pollution that was killing

our world. Things could have been so different for her and also the rest of us. If only she had reached out to someone a lot sooner... anyone. Maybe there are more like her who could, collectively, solve the energy and pollution crisis? Provide us all with a clean and even a free way to run everything? Although free is a bit much to hope for, isn't it? Who knows what secrets there are hidden away in the shadows or in the minds of these people? Unfortunately now she's dead now. Killed in an accidental fall while evading capture by security forces, I'm reliably informed. I'm sure that the whole truth will be hidden in the best interests of the national security for many years to come, possibly forever. Meanwhile, if there is anyone watching who does have this amazing ability, please try and use it for good. Seek out others like yourself and try and do something to save the planet instead of destroying it like Vera Castle tried to. Anyway, good people, friends of the channel and the thousands of my subscribers who keep everything ticking along, I'll be taking a break for a while but I can assure you I will be back to poke fun at politicians and pointless celebrities pretty soon. Until then I hope we can all get back to normal - whatever 'normal' is these days."

Steve, and most of the world, were oblivious to the threat Vera Castle had planned for the rest of mankind. Maybe that was the right decision by those who knew the truth to keep it classified. We all lived to fight another day... but for how long?

***

Well, that's the end of another book, and if you are reading this bit first then WHY? It's been around two years since the last one. There has been a lot of upheaval and health worries in my life over the last year which obviously delayed things a bit and it's hard to get motivated during all the turmoil with several things flying about inside my head at times although I did manage to get a bit done and even used the situation as a small bit of inspiration. People who know me also know the story but it's all worked out for the best and my life is pretty good now. I won't bore you with the details but I did get to experience a few new things, not all bad though. I did get a bit of (fictional) retribution on a couple of characters. Again, people who know me will spot them straight away and have a little chuckle at their demise. Karma is indeed a bitch.

So, now you should know I'm as far from a climate change nutter as I can possibly get. But I do recycle like the rest of us and do a fair bit of walking instead of driving. We can only do so much individually but as said in the story, its big business that is the problem. The amount of pollution they chuck out is staggering and governments turn a blind eye. The big question is WHY? Seems to me the whole world is corrupt but it's us ordinary people who foot the bill through taxation and ever escalating prices. And the biggest rises are thing we need to survive; food, water, gas and electricity. Fuel to transport food to shops and supermarkets is hit, as well as for us ordinary motorists, some of whom try to make a living on the road. People who drive from job to job. Good hardworking people. Grafters. We're all being forced off the roads with rising fuel prices, insurance hikes and even more taxation while the people who impose all this vote to give themselves a large pay rise every year. I doubt I could name more than two or three politicians who actually care about this country and the people. The rest are just in Parliament for what they can get. And it's the same in every country on the planet. Sorry to say it, but we are in for a very dystopian future the way things are going and there is very little time to reverse the process. What would it take though? Revolution, a World War? Who knows? Oops - that was a rant - anyway back to the book.

Obviously being a non-believer in the climate change tax hoax I found it surprising easy to put both sides across through certain characters. One or two were complete climate sheep including "Mother Earth". I tried to be quite sympathetic towards her mental illness though and tried to write her as someone who has had many issues throughout her life but firmly believed she was doing good, although she did kill more people than climate change ever will. I'm sure people like Mother Earth do exist, hopefully not with the kind of power she possessed but Telekinesis has been proven and then hijacked by the military and other nefarious organisations - you know the right combinations of the alphabet, don't you? Sometimes I think I would love to have her ability but I doubt I'd cause as much devastation as her... well, maybe just a little LOL.

I don't believe in any God but do believe in Nature and the main message of this book is how Nature will always survive in the end. Whether we will be around as a species is another matter, sometimes, like Mother Earth, I hope we aren't.

Natural disasters as depicted in the story have all happened in the past and will probably happen again. They really fascinate me, and I firmly believe that the earth goes through natural cycles, we've had a very long ice age, the planet has seen floods and droughts, plagues and even been hit by an asteroid which eradicated most of the life on the this planet, but some form of life will always survive whatever happens - maybe even all those corrupt politicians in their underground bunkers, which reminds me of the third book in the great James Herbert 'Rats' trilogy. In my opinion, the greatest ever British Horror writer, now sadly gone. I highly recommend his books for great 20th century Brit Horror. I doubt he'd recommend my books if he was still around because I know I'm definitely not in his class. But you, friends and readers, that's your job. Lend out a paperback to a friend or copy an ebook and send it to someone - let them read the books without spending their hard-earned cash. But as a lot of people know, I don't do this for the minute amount of money I get from any sales. I do it as a hobby, to entertain and as a form of relaxation and therapy (think of the ants)... and in the words of AC/DC "The names have been changed to protect the guilty".

*Disclaimer: All characters are a figment of my imagination.

I think I'm improving as a writer. I'm of the opinion that this is the best written book so far and a good Thesaurus definitely helps LOL. I think the pacing is a lot better this time but I think there are still issues with mixed tense and other things. I'm a work in progress. I truly believe that we should never stop learning and I'm doing my best to improve.

So to end on a positive note - all the trials and tribulations of the last year are now behind me and I'm happy for the first time in decades. I would like to thank all my friends who have helped me get through these difficult times (you all know who you are so I won't embarrass you by outing you all). Furniture donated, things stored for me, lifts all over the place or even a few kind words from people - it all meant so much to me and made me appreciate that some people do these things to be good people and not for what they can get out of it. Seems there may be hope for the human race, after all. Love you all.

Next to be published may be a collection of short stories (twelve started, one finished so far) or another full length novel - I'll be working on both at the same time as I have with this book.

Many thanks to everyone who have read this book, I know money is tight for most of us so it's appreciated, and if it's your first then please try out the others. I did manage to squeeze Mark Mason in this one but unfortunately not DI Gerry Daly, who is by far my favourite character from all the books. Rest assured, he will be back in the next novel.

As I write this the world is looking less secure by the day. We've had the Ukraine war for about eighteen months and now things are kicking off in the Middle East - I have my own thoughts on why this is all happening but will keep them to myself. Hopefully I'll sell a couple of copies of this book before WW3, LOL. I really hope for us all, and the planet, it never comes to that, but it's not our decision, is it?

Peace X

Also by Thomas J. Stone

A Rip in Time
Cast The First Stone
Second Chance: The Return of Anrok
*Reset Earth